Tracey Nowers

There's More to Me Than You

By Tracey Selanis Nowers

Eloquent Books

Eloquent Books
An imprint of Strategic Book Group
P.O. Box 333
Durham CT 06422
www.StrategicBookGroup.com

ISBN 978-1-60860-860-7

Printed in the United States of America

This book is dedicated to

Chatham and Kai, my two personal, ever-changing oceans.

Also, to my husband, Ed, who is the shelter in my storm.

"You know you can't hurt me forever;
I didn't sign up for you;"

> *– Goodbye Yellow Brick Road*
> *by Elton John*

Catherine, 1991

Chaos. White noise. It was like static on the radio; the noise in my head. The fainting spell returned, and I needed to pull my car over to rest a bit. My visibility was diminishing. After the worst of the feeling passed, I felt I was able to continue.

It was March in New England, and my Nissan was barely making it through the tall snow drifts that had formed. The storm last night had left the roads slick.

I could feel the sweat beading up on my forehead and saw white edging in on my peripheral vision. I was trying hard to focus and breathe deeply. The crackling sounds were coming from my chest, and I couldn't manage to take deep breaths. It was so scary, not knowing what was going on. But I did know one thing: it couldn't be good. I felt like I was drowning on air........

After what felt like an eternity and many rests on the side of the road, I finally saw the sign Franklin County Medical Center. Once I sloppily parked my car, I staggered in through the entrance and collapsed. I was not sure how long I was out, but when I came to, the emergency room doctor came in with my results: "You have some cracked ribs and a collapsed lung. We may need to take you to surgery if your lung doesn't start to repair itself in the next 24 hours. In the meantime, you need to stay in bed on oxygen therapy. The nurse will be in to get some information from you now that you are awake. Is there anyone you would like to call?" I was able to mutter "No" as my head reeled. *How did I get to this point? What the hell happened to my life?* Memories of the night before flooded my mind. *What did I do to deserve this? Is he sorry? Where will I go? I obviously can't stay with him. Do I have anyone I can call?* Then the realization hit: No, I had no one. I've been alone my whole life.

His last words to me hit hard. "I don't love you. No one will ever love you. I'm going to kill you." *I can't think about this now*, I told myself. I was crying which was making it so much harder to breathe. Blood pressure alarms went off on the monitor and the nurse came in. "You need to rest. This will help you sleep." Eventually I gave in as the sedative took effect. *Yes, I need to rest.* I had a whole lot of healing to do mentally and physically. But right now all I felt was as if I were untrusting, as if I were unlovable, and as if I had hit rock bottom.

Sleep took over although it was not restful.

Fear is heavy in the room. I'm hiding in the attic, in the way back, behind old bed springs and rockers. Thank god the light bulb has been blown out since last year. I don't dare even breathe, but my heart is pounding so loudly in my chest that I wonder if he can hear it. He is so close. He's screaming he's going to kill me. I feel like an animal being hunted. This is a humiliation I could never have imagined. I'm terrified and there's no way out. I used to stick up for myself, yell back, and shove back. When did I stop fighting? When did I become a victim? He's so angry and frustrated and has now started searching elsewhere in the house. I hear him pacing the floor down stairs, still screaming. I have no idea how I will ever get out of here. Minutes later, he comes back to search again and he sees my hiding spot. I hurdle boxes and old chairs. I'm almost at the stairs. I can hear him behind me. He pushes me from behind, and I land at the bottom of the attic stairs in a heap. I'm dazed and can't move quickly enough. He's bounding down the steps until he reaches my side. The first kick is the worst. I feel it make contact with my ribs, and it completely takes the wind out of me. Then I can feel him kicking me all over. From a distance, I can hear him screaming at me. He is saying hurtful, unspeakable things. Barely conscious, I feel his hands on my neck choking me. As I finally black out, all I can think is "Please just let me die."

I was screaming and inconsolable as the nurse came in to wake me. It was just another nightmare. Another flashback of that night. I've had a lot of those this week that I've been in the hospital. It turned out that I didn't need surgery. It seemed my body had fought and won. However, my mind had given in to him. He had won that battle. He had broken the spirit I had always prided myself on. I had been thinking about what I would do when I get out tomorrow. Maybe I would go back. I had nowhere else to go. I didn't really care what happened to me now.

He may as well finish me off. I had no place to live, a job that I hated, and no social support. He was right; I was unlovable. I was feeling this despair that I couldn't seem to shake. Maybe this was my fault. I didn't deserve any better. I was nothing.

Before my thoughts went any deeper, the social worker knocked on the hospital room door. *Gee, what tipped her off? Could it be the black and blues around my neck that were obviously left by fingers? Could it be the obvious lie about how I ended up here?* I assumed the staff must have to report any suspicious cases. She pulled up a chair, introduced herself, and asked about my injuries. I thought of all the possible things I could say, weighing my options. In the end, I decided to say nothing. I just couldn't tell anyone. Maybe it was pride. Maybe it was because I had lost my first battle of many in my life. Maybe I was just mentally and physically defeated.

"I slid into a snow bank. Thankfully my rubber bumper spared my car."

Recognizing the lie, she handed me her card as she left, in case I changed my mind. I bet she was used to this; the untold stories.

The humiliation I was feeling was so great; plus I still hadn't decided what to do and where to go. How could they possibly help me? I couldn't afford the first and last month's rent deposit to live on my own. I had looked into shelters in the past few weeks but I had no where to put my cat, which was like my baby. I had tried to move back home, but my parents weren't very supportive of that decision, although this situation may change their minds. I thought back to that night. It was ever present in my mind. All I knew was tomorrow, when I was discharged, was too soon for me to face the world or the rest of my life.

Sharon, 1970

The water had long since run lukewarm. I was still scrubbing my body to the point of bleeding, and I couldn't tell where my tears ended and the shower begun. I sank down against the wall of the shower as the shame inhabited my body. The silent sobs wrenched through me, and I couldn't stop them.

I'm dirty! Disgusting! I couldn't get clean enough; I couldn't block out the images. I trusted him! I was so stupid and naïve. I thought I was so mature at sixteen. My mom was right not to allow me to be alone with boys. If I told her what had happened, I couldn't imagine what my punishment would be. *I need to think. I need to think!* But right now all I could do was keep scrubbing. I needed to erase the evidence. I needed to erase my mind. I needed to forget this ever happened.

I was still scrubbing well after the water had turned cold, but my body didn't feel it. The scrubbing hadn't numbed my mind. The violation hadn't been erased or forgotten.

Catherine

It was over. It didn't even need to be discussed and wasn't. The fact that we had crossed some invisible line in our relationship was enough. He came to see me only once in the hospital. He didn't display any remorse. He brought a friend and couldn't stay because they were in a pool tournament, as if that wasn't a pathetic excuse.

I was being discharged from the hospital today. I had recovered well, being young and healthy. My lung had reattached itself. My body still ached, especially my ribs; and the black and blues that were turning yellow, were a constant reminder of my pitiful life.

Home. It made me wonder the true meaning. I had made a mess of my life. When I was younger, I was going to be rich and travel the world. I wasn't going to be married. I was used to using and abusing men. I thought that was what attracted me to Glenn. He was the only man I'd dated who wasn't intimidated by me. He took control, and it was nice to ease into the passenger seat for a while. Well, he took that control and little by little chipped away at me. My armor must have just been surface protection because it hadn't taken long to break me and make me dependent on him. Was that how I treated men before? But without the physical beating? I guess what goes around really does come back around.

I was noticing hints of sarcasm and irritability creeping into most thoughts now. I was being pulled to that negative, dark side, and at this point, I didn't care. It was not as if I had any one to impress at this point.

As I returned to the apartment for the first time since the fight, he looked at me coolly, "I'll stay with some friends while you move out." No how are you? The least he could have done was pick me up from the hospital. He was the one who had sent me there. I was not sure what I had expected, but it was certainly more than this.

I simply nodded in agreement with tears in my eyes. I wondered if he egotistically thought I was crying because of the breakup. In truth, it was hard to see him. I didn't feel anger although I had expected to. I felt so deeply hurt and vulnerable. Shocked. Exposed. No one else knew what had happened. As hard as I tried to deny it, it would change me forever.

He looked at me again straight in the eye. "I don't love you. No one could ever love you. You need to leave because one of these times I'm going to kill you." Then he left.

The shock of those words, said in all sincerity, not anger, was as bad as the beating. He knew how to cut me. I slid down the wall, sat on the floor, and promised myself that no one would get close to me again.

Sharon

As I awoke from my exhausted sleep after my shower, I could hear my mom rumbling around in the kitchen, starting supper. I got dressed. The more clothes I can put on, the more it'll hide the shame. I needed to act normal, I told myself, as I headed down to help my mom in the kitchen.

"Hi Mom!" I said a little too cheerfully.

"Hello, honey. How was your day?" she asked. I was on summer break and my mom had just returned from a Bible study session with some neighbors.

"Janie and I went to Godfrey's for root beer floats, and then I did some summer reading for next year," I lied.

"You're such a good girl. How did I get so lucky?" she smiled. I felt like disappearing. I hoped she didn't see me cringe.

"Can I help?" I asked, hoping to change the subject and forcing a smile. My father came home shortly thereafter and kissed each of us hello. My body jumped at the touch. He noticed that I had pulled away. I was the epitome of 'Daddy's Little Girl' and thrived on his attention.

"You gave me a static shock." I tried to recover when I saw the hurt on his face. "I'll go set the table." I quickly left the room.

I loved my parents. It was hard for me to keep this from them. I grew up an only child, and my parents doted on me. They were strict and protective of me and I always obeyed. We also moved a lot because my father was in the air force and it was hard to make and keep friends. My parents and I were close as they have been my primary and most stable friends.

Last year we moved to this small city in Rhode Island. There was talk of another transfer soon to Westover AFB in Chicopee, Massachusetts. Another school, new friends, and old ones left behind. I was getting to be a pro at goodbyes. After the first few teary moves, I decided to shut off the sad feelings and just go with the flow.

I was smart and had no trouble adjusting to the academics at the schools. I didn't like the extracurricular activities, but I did well when it came to book smarts. "All book smarts and no common sense," my father always said to me. At this particular moment, I believed him.

This place, however, was different from the other places we had lived. It was harder to fit in. I found I could reinvent whoever I wanted to be at each new place since they were usually short stays. Here I had decided to lay low. The cliques were impenetrable. I had one friend, Janie, but no boyfriend to speak of.

However, boys were starting to pay more attention to me now.

I was slowly becoming more comfortable with my developing body and exotic features. I was born in Hawaii and raised here in the continental United States. Dad met mom in the beginning of his career while serving in Hawaii. I got my looks from mom: slightly slanted eyes that are the color of espresso, olive skin, and long brown hair. My looks, coupled with how little people know about the "new girl" made people think I was mysterious. I also didn't act like the usual giddy high school girl. I acted as if I didn't care what they thought of me. All of this made me intriguing to boys and girls alike.

I was approaching a rebellious stage in my teenage years where I was often torn between liking the newly acquired attention from the boys and respecting my parents' strict upbringing. I was not allowed to date until I was seventeen, which was months away. I'd probably be at another part of the world by then the way my father moved us around.

Janie and I liked two particular boys and often watched them during lunch period. They were friends and equally adorable. We couldn't decide which one we liked better, since we have never spoken to them. One day they had lunch with us and asked if they could walk us home. Unsure if that would be okay, we hesitantly said no. After that, we spent a couple weeks flirting back and forth on school grounds only. Janie and I had finally decided we would let them walk us home, but on that particular day, she ended up having to stay late to help a teacher. I ended up walking with them alone, feeling a little wicked, and feeling relieved Janie wasn't there, so I could have all their attention.

Maybe I'd finally decide whom I liked better. We talked about different places I had lived and how long I'd be staying in town. We made eye contact a few times, and I had butterflies. I had never been the center of attention like this, and I was thoroughly enjoying it. It made me more bold and flirtatious. When we got to my house, I thanked them and said, "I'll see you at school Monday."

One of them asked, "Can I use the bathroom?"

"I can't have anyone in the house while my parents are gone. My mom is helping the church set up for a dance. Sorry," I said uncertainly.

"Please. I have to pee." I felt silly not letting this boy that I knew use the bathroom.

"Uh, okay," I stammered. Mike and I waited in the kitchen while John went upstairs to the bathroom. While trying to fill the uncomfortable silence, he commented on the woodwork of our house. With the crown molding and pocket doors, this house definitely stood out. We lived in an old Victorian house, and it was built with only one bathroom upstairs. This was the only house I've ever seen with one bathroom on the second level. We had antiques we've collected from all over the world, and they went nicely in these old, wallpapered rooms. I had always appreciated the character of older houses, especially the ones with a story to them. In particular, the kitchen has always been my favorite room in the house, and my mom and I often baked pies here.

After a few seconds Mike said, "Hey." and as I turned to look at him, he kissed me straight on the lips. I was stunned. I could feel the warmth of his breath and the pressure from his lips. I pulled away.

"What's the matter? You don't like me?" he asked teasingly.

"No, I do, really," I insisted. Just then, John came down.

"Are you ready to go?" They said goodbye and headed home.

That was the first encounter we had after school. They had become more frequent, and continued into the summer, after school had let out for the completion of my sophomore year. They were more frequent and daring on my part. I had become obsessed with the attention and took a particular liking to Mike. We had been kissing and I even let him touch my breasts. My teenage body was awakening under his touch. Everything was new to me, and I couldn't get enough. Sometimes in church, after confession, I'd feel guilty for the way I was feeling.

Although I did want him to like me, I was trying not to get too attached. We were bound to be moving soon, and I tried to convince myself that this was normal teenage lust. However, being as immature as I was, I started to confuse his attention with love. I was hungry for it. I never said no to his fumbling fingers. We were learning together. It wasn't a public relationship. I still wasn't allowed to date. We never went out anywhere together. It was all clandestine meetings, and I loved having a secret. Mostly we'd go to an old wooden shed in the woods behind my house. We met a few times a week for a few months. One day, I was waiting for him in the shed, and he walked in with John. I was disappointed. I was looking forward to spending time with him, and now we had company. I had even daringly gone without a bra to make easy access. Sometimes it took him forever to undo the clasp!

"Hey," John said. Mike came over and kissed me full on the mouth. His tongue parted my lips and searched out mine. My desire for him heightened. As uncomfortable as I was with John looking on, it was also intense as we had never been public about our affections.

"Do you mind if he stays?" Mike whispered in my ear.

"What do you mean?" I stammered.

"He's having a hard time making a move on his girlfriend, and I said you'd help me show him how easy it is. C'mon, you don't mind do you?"

"I'd feel a little funny-that's all," I said meekly. I was torn between doing this and possibly losing Mike as my boyfriend if I didn't. School and my life here had been almost unbearably boring until we had met. I wanted to keep the excitement going while I could. *What was the big deal anyway?* Mike sensed my hesitation.

"How about if I blind fold you? You wouldn't even know he was here. It would be kind of neat." I hesitantly agreed. John pulled off his bandana and Mike tied it around my head. He backed me up against the old wooden workbench and started kissing my neck. It was sending chills down my spine. I was starting to relax under his touch. His breath was hot on my skin. He inched my shirt up and started making circles with his tongue around my nipples. My nipples had always been sensitive and were rock hard. I was arching my body and aching for him to just take my nipple in his mouth. I was feeling a warm tickle starting to spread in my belly and could feel the wetness seeping through my panties. Will we ever get to third base? Should I let him? Finally, he was taking my breast in his mouth. He was sucking harder. I couldn't get enough. I knew I shouldn't be doing this, which was what made it all the more exciting. I could feel his hardness against me through our clothes. *What would it be like?* The anticipation was killing me! I could feel his fingers travel down to my wetness, exploring, probing.

"Uhmmmm," the moan escaped my throat. I felt like his hands were all over my body. It felt incredible. Little did I realize it was because John had joined in the fun.

"Get down on all fours!" Mike demanded. Hmmm- something new, I thought. Next thing I knew his dick was in my face.

"Suck it!" I took it in my mouth. It was small and tasted sweet. *This wasn't bad,* I thought. In the next moment I was shocked to feel my skirt pushed up, panties ripped off, and a tongue licking my private parts.

"What…?"

"Just relax," John said.

"You might like it. I hear you like everything." My body was on guard but when I felt his tongue on certain parts of my body, the sensation was out of this world. I was becoming a woman. I was ashamed that I liked how this felt. The very core of me knew this was wrong, but I didn't want it to stop.

"Lay down," Mike instructed. As curious and excited as I was, I felt we had done enough for the day. I was becoming uncomfortable and wasn't prepared to do anymore. Plus, Janie was interested in John. I was sure she wouldn't approve of him being here.

"I think I should get home," I stated defiantly. The next thing I knew I was flipped over on my back. I was disoriented since I was still blind folded. One of them straddled my chest and put his dick in my mouth to quench my screams.

"I have a camera and I'll post pictures of you at church and school if you don't suck me off until I come. Then I want to fuck you like Mike's going to do. Got it, babe? You know you want it. You've been begging for it for months." I froze. I didn't think things would go this far. Terrified, I nodded, tears running down my cheeks. *It wasn't supposed to be like this.* Just then, Mike slammed into me. I felt the sharp pain and cringed. John slapped me in the head.

Mike came pretty quickly, thank god. John pulled out and came all over my face. He ripped the bandana off just before so I could watch him beaming down, enjoying his powerful moment. They were hard again right away being so young and virile. They were caught up in the moment and were almost unrecognizable as the boys I thought I knew. They switched, and John lasted longer, raping me with no regard to my whimpers. Mike was sweating, his face contorted as he came in my mouth. John was still inside me from behind and started penetrating my anus with his finger. The pain was unbearable. I knew I had caused this. I had asked for it and taken pleasure in most of it. Finally done with me, they left me there with my shame.

Catherine

I planned on spending the week looking for supplemental income and packing what little I own. I was a waitress at a small town restaurant with meager tips. His parents owned the apartment we shared and the rent was cheap. I didn't have enough for first, last, and security. I was getting desperate. My thoughts bounced around. *Should I just ask to stay?* Maybe he wouldn't do it again. We'd go back to being just roommates. It was the only easy solution I could come up with as I had too much emotional baggage to think things through and to make a rational decision. Everything seemed like too much work at this point. I didn't even want to get up in the morning. Not because I missed him. I just didn't want to face the world. And still his words kept echoing in my head, "No one will ever love you."

I was adopted. He knew this bothered me. I couldn't under-stand how someone could abandon their child. The circumstances didn't matter, just being loved by your parents and being together was what is important. My birth mother gave me up after a couple weeks. She never wanted me but did give it a try. She gave me up to an orphanage. It's been a black mark on my life ever since and he successfully used it against me.

I was adopted by a Polish couple after spending only two days at the orphanage. They were hard working and provided the necessities. I spent my life trying to be the perfect daughter to repay them for giving me a home. In turn they felt no need to dote or pay much attention since I was so self-sufficient. We never bonded as parents and child should, and I went through life with this emptiness. Nothing could fill the void. Not good grades, scholarships, beauty pageants, sports or popularity. I was still searching for the peace that only love can bring.

I was on the floor, still crying, holding Chuckie, my cat. I thought back. Glenn and I met through mutual friends. I had just graduated from high school and before going off to college, I spent the summer with friends at the lake. We spent every day water-skiing. It was my passion. I was confident on the water as I cut and sprayed. Everyday I longed to get out on the millpond and exhaust every muscle. I was a natural. That's what attracted him to me. I believe he saw a challenge to conquer. Two high-strung, cocky people are never a good mix. We flirted over margaritas with friendly jibes back and forth. Then the summer was over and it was time to head to college. I had already taken entrance exams and courses were picked. Right before I left, my mom let me know she had withdrawn me over the summer and could not help with the fees. I had worked my whole life for this. I had straight A's, was in the top tenth of my class, was voted most likely to succeed, and had broken records in track and field. I had turned down volleyball scholarships to other schools. I was devastated. To me, there was never a possibility of NOT going to college. It was too late. They had already given away the dorm and classes. Coincidentally, I now needed a place to live, and he needed a roommate. I was too angry to stay at home. We decided I would move in as friends. I kept my own bedroom for almost a year.

One hot summer night, he decided it was time I learned to do a true tequila shot. I would impress the men with this, he said. First, you licked the salt, let it sit in your mouth a bit while the saliva formed, did the shot and then the lemon. You actually didn't even need the lemon. You didn't taste the tequila as it was so coated by saliva on the way down.

Well, the heat and the tequila had its effect, and we became lovers. I don't know if we just wanted companionship, or if we were just bored, or if this was convenient, but the anticipation of that moment had been growing over the last year.

We went through the usual nervousness of a beginning relationship. On our first actual date, he accidentally locked the keys in the car. After some time, we bought a couch together. That was a huge step for me. For my birthday, he bought me a diamond Claddagh ring. Things were going comfortably well for a while, and then it changed as all relationships eventually do. We spent more time apart, had separate friends, and separate interests. We even stopped having sex. Neither of us seemed to mind. He would make comments that were always disapproving. Before long, I was feeling as if I couldn't do anything right. When he started to come home in other women's cars that was the last straw. He'd be late and drunk. Our fights were loud, and neither of us would back down. We were in unspoken competition over who could be more pig headed and stubborn. Over time it escalated. We would push each other's buttons easily, and I think we secretly enjoyed the power we had to unsaddle the other.

One time the two of us were at the lake; it was Super Bowl Sunday. We were playing one- on-one ice hockey. Competitive as always, he got mad when I scored and "accidentally" checked me hard. When my head hit the ice, I heard him laugh before I lost consciousness. I also thought I heard him say "I hope you're dead." But I never knew for sure if my mind was playing tricks on me.

I woke up in the hospital being treated for a mild concussion and hypothermia. Friends and family assumed he had taken me there. I learned he had left me there, and I was found by other skaters hours later. I was a statistic. Domestic violence is higher on Super Bowl than on any other day of the year. It should have been a wake up call. I just thought I was foggy and unclear about what happened. And now this....

Sharon

We moved shortly after to Thorndike, a village in Palmer, in western Massachusetts. It was not far from Chicopee where my dad was posted and was situated on the outskirts of the Quabbin Reservoir. The Quabbin was known for its history of the flooding of four towns to create a drinking reservoir for the city of Boston and its surrounding towns. Although beautiful, it was really very sad to see the crumbling foundations and pieces of dishes still there as proof of those families that existed before they were run out of their own homes and close-knit communities. Squire Street, where we lived, was picturesque with the Elm tree-lined streets and rocking chairs on the front porches.

I had finished the summer in Rhode Island mostly alone. I was numb. I was hollow. I didn't speak to anyone, not even Janie. Mostly, I just slept the day away in deep depression. My parents were worried but thought things would get better once we moved. Maybe new surroundings would cure me.

After we settled into the new house and before the start of school, my mom did the usual stuff like establish doctors and dentists and sign me up for my junior year of school. I needed a physical for enrollment, and it was time for a checkup anyway. We went to Dr. Miller at Westover AFB who told my mom I was going through normal teenage stuff and the phase would pass. Every thing else checked out okay. "Give it some time," he said. "She needs to adjust from the move."

My mom refused to let me sleep my life away and enlisted my help later that week.

"Please pack up these cookies for our neighbors, Sharon." I dutifully packed them up and delivered them next door. I rang the door bell.

"Hi!" I looked up to see a boy about my age standing on the other side of the door. He wasn't particularly good looking but had a nice smile.

"I was wondering when I would meet you. I had heard there were new neighbors with a daughter. I'm Peter. What's your name?"

"I'm Sharon," I said simply, not in the mood to make small talk.

"Are you sick or something?" He was referring to my sunken eyes and pale skin that didn't seem to go with the beautiful summer weather. True, I hadn't been out and about much.

"No, just tired lately."

"Would you like to come in?" he asked. We got acquainted while we stood in his foyer. He seemed nice enough. He had lived here in Palmer his whole life. He was very interested in hearing about the different places I had lived. After I met his parents and gave them the cookies, I went back to my house. I was tired.

"You met our neighbor?" Mom asked, a little too hopeful.

"Yeah," and I went to my room to sleep away my troubles.

Catherine

I had desperately looked for a place to live after our breakup. I needed money fast and time was running out. After seeing an ad, I swallowed my pride (what was left of it after being beat up) and applied to the only place I could get money fast, easy, and a lot of it. I rode one and one-half hours to a strip club in Springfield. I have no idea what I was thinking when I walked into that dark, urine-smelling club. I had already hit rock bottom, and this was nothing compared to that. I filled out an application and was introduced to the manager. I was instructed to take my clothes off so he could see if I was firm enough for the job. He also wanted to see if I had any rhythm or if I could dance seductively. Standing there with only a G-string in front of him, I realized I was giving another man power over me again. I grabbed my clothes and ran out of his office. After vomiting in the dressing rooms, I sped home. I started packing immediately. I was desperate, I was scared, and I needed to get the hell out of this place that held so many bad memories. I packed up my car, with my cat and clothes, and drove to the biggest city I could lose myself in: Washington D.C.

I had always wanted out of our small town. College wasn't happening; and since my abusive relationship, it was a good time to leave. I needed to find out who I was, to reestablish some dreams, and to just be alone. I made contact with an old friend in Northern Virginia. He and I had dated in high school and remained friends. His family moved after our junior year. They welcomed me to join them in Northern Virginia, in a town called Reston, until I found a place and a job. Shahram and his family were so hospitable to me that it was hard to consider ever leaving. They were Iranian, and I found myself in the language and customs. I was slowly picking up Farsi, their language. Ata, his father, was part owner of a dry cleaning company and worked very hard for his family. Their family name was very well known in Tehran before they fled during the war. Giti, his wife, was a hair dresser, and she did a great job managing the four boys. The food was amazing. The tea was strong. I was hooked. The rice and spices were tantalizing. My favorite dishes were Loubia Pollo: Minced lamb, green beans in a tomato, and lime sauce and also steamed chicken, saffron, and barberries over rice. We had radishes and onions on the side that we ate like apples. The baklava was perfect except for the rose water. All the desserts had rose water. It made the food taste like roses smell. I attended elaborate dinners at other houses and weddings. Their music was my music; their dance was mine.

Life was very comfortable and before I knew it, six months had gone by. Shahram and I picked up where we left off, as friends. We could always talk about things. We spent many nights with a beer and deep conversation. He told me when we dated he never felt as though he could get close to me, he felt as if he could never break down my walls. We talked about how intimidating I was to boys in high school and how he respected how strong and unconquerable I was. I cried when I told him how weak I was and that I did indeed get conquered. It was the first time I had spoken of the beating. He had seen a difference in me and sensed something was wrong. On nights he had heard me crying, he would come into my room and sing me to sleep. It was very tempting to halt time and stay like that but I was getting restless now. I decided I needed to do something with my life. I didn't want to think about where I had been and all my failed plans. It was time to get back to basics. What did I enjoy? What did I want to do with the rest of my life? That question was answered the next morning.

I started each day with a strong cup of tea and the newspaper. Finally, one ad stood out:

Dog Walker needed for busy kennel
Mature Person needed for weekends only
Please apply in person to
between the hours of 9:00 am – 4:00pm
Reston Animal Hospital
2403 Reston Parkway

This was a place I could walk to it was so close! I applied and was delighted to get hired. I really enjoyed the time with the dogs. They were so forgiving and happy at the simplest things. How could they not be uplifting and therapeutic? They just gave unconditional love ....and no talking back. I was able to open my heart again, just a little, to something safe.

My job also entailed cleaning the kennel runs and cat cages, feeding, bathing and medicating. Sometimes I would help restrain animals for the doctors and technicians. My heart broke when I witnessed a euthanasia performed by the veterinarian. The cat was so thin and frail. The owner was sobbing, grief-stricken, over the cat's lifeless body. I offered what little comfort I could to her. In that moment, it solidified what I wanted to do: I wanted to work with these amazing pets and owners for the rest of my life.

I also started working at the Gap during the week. I was good at sales and could understand the foreign conversations of the many Iranians who shop there. When they were hesitant about a purchase, I told them, "Gashanghe!" *It looks good.* I was also meeting new people outside of the Iranian circuit. We'd get together to go dancing in DuPont Circle and Georgetown, to the movies, or just hang out and watch 60 minutes on Friday nights.

I had finally saved enough money and located a place to sublet for 9 months. It was a small loft in a townhouse not far from DuPont Circle in D.C. I transferred Gap stores but changed to limited weekends only. I was working at a small government office helping translate Farsi to English, a job Ata helped me get. I also walked dogs on the weekend for a local shelter in D.C. I didn't mind the many hours and was saving up some money, but

I was alone. Although, I knew some acquaintances through work, I hadn't made any true friends since moving into the city. With all my jobs, it was hard to have the time to see friends from Virginia. All I have is my two cats: Chuckie, whom I brought with me, and Peeshe. Peeshe means kitten in Farsi. He was found in the dumpster behind the Reston Animal Hospital. They were my lifeline.

Sharon

I started my new school but this time there was no effort in a charade. I was subdued. I never smiled. I didn't make honor roll and even failed some classes. I kept to myself for the most part except for walking to and from school with my neighbor, Peter. It seemed funny that my parents were okay with this. Little did I know, they were desperate to have their old daughter back and would welcome anything to bring back the normalcy of our household.

Peter Szaban was a nice guy. He got average grades and was friendly with the other kids. But mostly, he was a loner like me. He always seemed to be holding something back. We were drawn to each other because we had this in common and our parents were always together so it seemed natural that we would always be together. He was the one who maintained the friendship. It was completely platonic. Although I knew everything about him, he knew very little about me. I let him take the lead because I was still unresponsive and broken inside.

I continued to sleep a lot and my mother could not shake the feeling that something was wrong. She asked me constantly and my response was always "I'm fine." It wasn't long before she phoned the doctor again.

When I was at the doctor's office the last time, he had asked me if I was sexually active. If front of my mom, I had, of course, answered no. That question sparked a thought in me that I hadn't been able to shake: *How long had it been since I had my last period?* It had been over 3 months since I was overpowered by John and Mike on that summer afternoon. Just thinking about it, turned my stomach. I hadn't allowed myself to think of that day or anything related to that day or that place.

Suddenly, it was so clear. I did feel really tired during the whole move. Was it the adjustment?

I had gained a paunchy stomach, but I attributed that to my lazy lifestyle. I didn't like to exercise and I had been lying down more than usual. Plus with the holidays approaching......

But I hadn't had my period in months.

I had been denying the obvious but something needed to be done soon. Having a baby so young and out of wedlock was out of the question in this day and age, especially to the church.

What was I going to do?

Marrying the father was not possible. I didn't even know which of them the father was! Having the baby was not an option. I didn't want any reminders of that night. I had heard there are places that help women get rid of babies. Places I wouldn't know

how to get to. They do black magic there and some people make
it and some don't.

Ohmigod, ohmigod, ohmigod...

Panic was spreading through me.

What do I tell my parents? My life is ruined. I don't want 'it'.

I'll never want this evil seed they planted. Never!

Catherine

As time went on, my confidence slowly started to return and my abusive past seemed a world away. It was hard for me to even remember. It had happened to another person. The months went by and it was the same routine. I got up, exercised, and grabbed a coffee for the walk to work. Traffic in the city sucked. I had found driving and walking the same distance takes an equal amount of time. On weekends, I took the train to the shelter. I did what needed to be done and headed home.

One afternoon at the Gap, the monotony of my life was interrupted. I looked up to see the most gorgeous man I had ever seen walk through the door. He had tan skin, wavy hair, and a perfect build. If ever I believed there was a God, he was it. After giving him a few minutes to look and gathering up my courage, I asked if he needed help. He said, "Maybe," and we made small talk. He had a beautiful smile and smelled delicious. We flirted; I made clothing suggestions. While he was in the fitting room, I couldn't wipe the silly smile off my face. He came out to model one outfit. The tan chinos fit well. His thighs were muscular, and he had no problem filling out those pants everywhere. The white, European cut, button down shirt was a nice offset to his tan. His chest hair peeked out at the buttons, just enough to make me want to follow it down.....

"What do you think?" he asked, interrupting my daydreaming.

"I think it's perfect. Any special occasion?" I asked.

"For my date with you tonight," He replied. And so I went. It had been so long since I had been with a man or had any company. I wore a casual tan linen dress suit. He took me to dinner in Georgetown. The Italian restaurant was authentic with dim lighting, beautiful tablecloths, and excellent food. The conversation was playful with many sexual innuendos. His looks and touch were spreading warmth throughout my body. It had been almost a year since I had been with anyone. We held hands as we lingered over our after dinner drinks: amaretto with floating coffee beans. We declined dessert. We couldn't make it to the apartment fast enough. He lived nearby. His apartment was masculine. He was into art deco, by the look of it. I barely remember as we fiercely kissed before we made it in the door. There was nothing slow and tender about this. I needed him, I needed human contact, and he was willing to oblige. Somehow we made it onto his bed. My juices were pouring out of me. One look at this man had me aroused and now his hands were all over me. I couldn't contain myself. I came hard just licks after his tongue searched me out. I needed to feel him inside me now! He filled me, and the warmth spread throughout my body. I was getting lighter and lighter, and now the rush was building again. I arched to meet his every thrust. His skin was salty, and he spoke softly to me. He was quite a man and had only skimmed the tip of my hunger. I came again with him, and he collapsed on top of me. He fell asleep shortly after, and I slipped out of the bed to head home.

Sharon

Later that week, I asked my mom if we could go to the mall in Springfield. She was excited I was showing an interest in anything so it was pretty easy to get her to take me. We needed to do Christmas shopping anyway. We spent the day there shopping and having lunch. While there, I went to some clothes stores. I couldn't help picking out plain, oversized outfits to match my mood and figure. My mom seemed surprised at my choice in clothing and the fact that I hadn't modeled anything outside the dressing room. She approached my sullenness on the drive home.

"I made an appointment with the doctor to recheck you. It's next week"

"Mom, I'm fine."

"Maybe so, but I have this feeling that something is wrong and you obviously aren't talking to us about it. Are you upset about the move? You've always been so well-adjusted. Sometimes we don't consider how you must feel. Anyway, you know you can come to us -about anything. Or you can talk to the doctor or our pastor, right?" Both she and my father had tried several times to get me to open up to them. I think anger was starting to take the place of concern since I had never distanced myself from them before. Was this normal teenage stuff or was it more serious?

"Yes, Mom." In the meantime, I was dreading the appointment for next week. I didn't have the strength to know the truth. I didn't want to face it.

In my heart, I already knew.

Catherine

It was snowing today and the city pretty much closed down for an inch of snow. I had never understood that, being from New England. I had the day to myself and headed to the quad. I loved the monuments and museums and had missed the feel of the crunch of the snow beneath my feet. I welcomed the cold. I turned my face toward the sky and let the snow fall on my face. It was quiet. I think it was the first time the city had been quiet. Or maybe it was the first time I had listened.

I felt so different from the girl I was when I left Massachusetts. Looking back, it was as if I were someone else. I couldn't even identify with the insecurities I had felt then. I had grown and still had a lot more to do. I found I was not strong enough to be in a relationship yet and was still submissive to men, even those I worked with. I had learned to never depend on a man for anything. The only person I could count on was myself. I had made strong advances in my confidence but knew it was a never-ending battle.

In the past year, I had learned quite a bit about myself: I was not a people person. I loved animals. I was a vegetarian in my heart but loved the taste of a good steak with a glass of merlot. I loved to read and was intrigued with foreign culture. Was that enough to build on? It would have to be for now.

I don't know when I made the conscious decision, but I started to make plans to leave the city. My sublet would be up in one month and was not available for renewal. I applied for a job transfer posted at the shelter for full time work at an animal shelter on Cape Cod. I was going back to my roots, back to Massachusetts. I would like being near the ocean. I would love not having to lock my doors with three dead bolts and carry mace. Things were happening.

Sharon

"Hello, Sharon. Your mom wants me to examine you alone today. Just in case you feel more comfortable without her present. How are things going?" Dr. Miller asked. It was obvious she had filled him in before we even arrived.

"Fine," I managed.

"How are you adjusting in your new school?"

"Fine."

"Are there any concerns you have? Anything that you'd like to discuss? Maybe your diet or bathroom habits?"

"Not really."

"Why don't you sit on the exam table and we'll get started."

I eased myself up on the table, rigid with fear. Dr. Miller looked at my mouth, throat, eyes, and ears and listened to my chest.

"All right, lie back while I palpate your abdomen and check reflexes, please." I did as I was told and closed my eyes tight. He was kneading my abdomen which was only slightly sticking up under the gown.

"Do you have regular periods, Sharon?"

"Usually."

"This is really important, Sharon. When was your last period?" He asked very seriously. I started crying.

"I don't know. A while, I guess. Please help me."

Dr. Miller helped me sit up and got me some tissues.

"I'd like to do a pelvic exam, Sharon, to see if you're definitely pregnant and to try to tell how far along you are. Is that okay? I'm assuming you're no longer a virgin." I shook my head. I didn't feel as though I had a choice. The truth would be out soon.

"Would you like your mom here?" he asked. I shook my head no!

After the exam, which was uncomfortable, I was cried out and feeling numb. It was very humbling to have a doctor look at my privates like that. He was now talking to my mother in his office as I was getting dressed. I felt as if everyone, including the nurse, was staring at me as I went to the waiting room. The waiting seemed like an eternity.

Finally, the door to the office opened, and my mother came out. She wouldn't even look at me. She kept her eyes down and kept walking to the car. I followed her out obediently. She said nothing the whole ride home. I knew she was going to be talking to dad before confronting me. She never did anything without discussing it with him. It was a very long, uncomfortable ride. I didn't dare move. I wanted to be invisible.

Catherine

I had driven out to Cape Cod to look at the shelter that I would be running. It was a long drive and I took my time. I drove through Buzzards Bay and stopped at the Canal to appreciate it. It was unbelievable that it was dug out by hand and the sand hauled away by wheel barrels. I vowed to get some roller blades once I was settled so I could join those who looked so carefree skating down the sides of the canal.

I was lucky enough to see the railroad bridge go down. It came down for a train to pass over it. It would have made a great picture if I had my camera handy. I saw a barge and tugboat fight against the current, hauling oil. Men were fishing off the sides of the canal, some with rods and others with lobster traps. But the smell was what really got my attention. It was heavy with salt and mist. It's hard to explain. I think you either loved it or hated it, but I was hooked.

The MSPCA shelter needed a lot of TLC, but I was up for the challenge. I had some ideas to implement a pairing program for pets and owners: a screening process that would help ensure a good and lasting fit for adoption. The staff was wonderful and welcoming. I was shown my soon-to-be office, and one of the girls gave me a run down on the area attractions.

I was excited about the move. I felt I would fit in here while I never felt at home in D.C.

I looked at some rentals, and there were some possibilities. I also left word with the other shelter employees and volunteers that I was looking. Spring and summer rentals are highly inflated, and I was worried about what I would have to pay. I would love to move just once but had to consider doing a summer rental then moving to a winter rental as many of the cottages were seasonal only. My hopes of being within walking distance of the ocean quickly diminished as I learned this.

I did stop to see the ocean again on the last day before returning home even though it was late winter and very brisk. It was low tide, and I happened upon a beach called Mayflower in Dennis. I walked out for what seemed like miles and explored tidal pools made up of sea worms, sand dollars, and crabs. I didn't want to leave, but I was nervous the tide would come in quickly. It was near sunset so I climbed up the lifeguard chair, and I just sat there staring. I felt so small and insignificant next to the ocean's vastness. There was a calmness that set in the longer I sat there, and I knew: I was home.

There was a saying: once you get Cape Cod sand beneath your feet, you never want to leave. This is exactly where I needed to be. I would never leave. I was officially a Cape Cod Wash-a-Shore.

Sharon, Jan 1971

We got through Christmas with a fake effort at normalcy and didn't speak about my pregnancy. I almost wondered if my parents needed that time to calm down before we discussed it. We had a family meeting with the pastor of our church that Sunday after the service. I was almost relieved to have it out in the open. The secret was out. I had lived with the unknown of what their reaction would be eating away at me for weeks. I was now in my second trimester. Dr Miller had confirmed it.

We had dinner in the formal dining room with Mom's best china. It was an obvious attempt to show we were well-to-do under these horrible circumstances. We ate pot roast cooked to perfection with candied sweet potatoes and had pumpkin pie for dessert. It appeared to be just an ordinary Sunday dinner, but it was the first time Mom and I didn't bake the pie together.

My stomach had been in knots all week, anticipating this. I couldn't choke down a bite of food. *Why doesn't someone say something?!* It was only after we cleared the table and retired into the sitting room that the subject was broached.

"Pastor, as you know we had moved from Rhode Island this fall. We have recently found out Sharon had gotten into a bad predicament prior to our move. My wife and I have discussed it and are looking to seek God's faith in our decision. We would like to have your help."

"Of course, Mr. and Mrs. Dent. Please go on."

"She is with child and is due in May. She will be turning 17, and she is not wed. We understand the church's rules about having children out of wedlock. We seek God's forgiveness."

"Let us pray together." We had always been a religious family. Not only was I afraid of losing my parents; I was also afraid of losing the church. This had been our stability as a family. This was where we were first welcomed after each move. This was where we make our acquaintances. It was also where we were at peace. Except for the last months, I had always felt accepted and loved and now I felt shame.

After we prayed, Father blessed me and asked me to come to confession and then meet with him for spiritual counseling twice weekly. They continued to speak of me as if I were not there.

"We have decided to help raise the baby as our own." My parents replied.

"No!" I cried, unable to sit quiet any longer.

"Sharon, control yourself. We are helping you," my father said sternly, clearly embarrassed by my outburst.

"I don't want a baby, especially not this baby!" I screamed.

"Is there a chance the baby's father will wed Sharon? Does he know about the baby?" the pastor asked.

"We hadn't discussed that with her yet. Sharon, we need to know who the baby's father is."

Catherine, Spring 1991

I started packing. I didn't have much to pack really, but it seemed overwhelming to me. Actually, everything was taking its toll on me. I was beyond irritable and emotional. I made dinner plans with the Fatemis to have my last taste of Iranian food before leaving and to say goodbye. They were celebrating their Haft Sin, their new year. Haft Sin or the seven Ss was a major tradition of Nowruz. The Haft Sin table included seven specific items starting with the letter S or *Sin* (س) in the Persian Alphabet. Items on the table symbolically correspond to seven creations and holy immortals protecting them. The items included:

sabzeh – wheat, barley or lentil sprouts growing in a dish – symbolizing rebirth

samanu – a sweet pudding made from wheat germ – symbolizing affluence

senjed – the dried fruit of the Oleaster tree – symbolizing love

sīr – garlic – symbolizing medicine

sīb – apples – symbolizing beauty and health

somaq – sumac berries – symbolizing the color of sunrise

serkeh – vinegar – symbolizing age and patience

We had all of my favorite foods: chicken on long grain rice pancakes with saffron and barberries and a cucumber, tomato, onion salad. I helped get the tea and baklava after dinner. I was tired and flushed from the visiting, gift exchange, dancing, and reminiscing. I would truly miss this: the song, the language, the closeness of this family. They had opened up their home and hearts to me when I needed it most.

Giti asked, "Are you leaving because of the child?"

"I'm sorry?" I asked, not knowing what she was saying.

"Oh........nothing. Are you sad to be leaving?"

We spoke some more, but I was distracted by my thoughts. I had an odd sensation that started in the kitchen that I couldn't shake. I was trying to figure out what Giti had said or what she was trying to say. It stayed with me the rest of the night.

It was a few days later when it struck me again-the oddity of her statement.

Catherine

Okay.....where are you? I was as regular as they come. I could tell you my period would start on a Monday morning at 10:30 am, and it would. Well, it was Wednesday night and I was two and one-half days late!

I couldn't be pregnant. I haven't even been with anyone but Marc and that was ....almost 3 weeks ago. I ran to the calendar. Let's see I was due on March 12. My last period was February 12. It was now March 14, and I was supposed to move later this spring! I broke into a full sprint to my purse, grabbed some cash, and ran to the corner drug store. I stared at the kit for a full hour before getting the courage to use it. I had to think rationally before I took it. *I just couldn't be. It's the stress of the move.*

If I am?... I have never wanted to get married or have kids. What was I going to do with a kid? I have stayed away from them like a plaque my whole life. I went into my tiny bathroom, peed on the stick, left the room and guzzled a beer in an act of defiance. After exactly five minutes, I reentered the bathroom, looked at the stick, and started laughing.

Sharon

I didn't return to Palmer High School. I never completed my junior year. I had flunked it anyway. My rank was 186 out of 186. Boy! Did my life do a turn around!

I had the baby on May 7, 1971. I delivered at the Westover AFB Hospital in Chicopee, MA. The labor went fast with my being so young and otherwise healthy. I was seeing a light at the end of the tunnel. This nightmare would be over soon. Little did I know; it was just the beginning. Caring for an infant was hard work.

My only visitor other than my parents was Peter. He and I had continued to be friends even after finding out about my condition. He was my only link to the outside world. I had pretty much stayed home during the obvious months of my pregnancy. Rumor was that I was ill. My father requested a transfer so that we could start in a new town as a young widow with a baby who had moved back with her parents. He was trying to save the family name.

Peter and I had an easy friendship, but we never got too involved with my details. He knew I was pregnant but never asked how or with whom. Therefore, he never passed judgment on me. I was beginning to feel comfortable and safe with him. Something I had never thought I would feel again. He never even looked at me like a blossoming young woman. I just assumed he only thought of me in a platonic way. Truth was he had his own inner turmoil to deal with. It would be a long time before he told me about it.

The baby was a girl. She had a whole lot of black hair with olive skin. I was able to avoid holding her initially feigning I was tired from the labor. The nurses and my mother had to get a little tough with me, and finally I nursed her. She cooed and ate well then fell asleep comfortably in my arms. She appeared so innocent and looked up at me as if I were her whole world. Funny though… I felt nothing for this child.

Catherine

The laughing turned into hysterical sobs and violent shaking. Two lines! Two! I was pregnant. All the symptoms and Giti's statement came to me. I should have known. I didn't even feel the need to repeat the test.

I leaned against the wall and cursed fate. I was turning into my biological mother, the person I hated most in this world. History was repeating itself. However, I could choose abortion, whereas it wasn't a legal option for my mother. Roe vs. Wade wasn't passed until 1972.

I couldn't say I was confused about what to do. I didn't even allow myself to consider this a baby.

I didn't want this baby. No part of me wanted it, and I never considered keeping it.

I wouldn't put it through adoption because I didn't believe a child could ever shake the fact that he/she were abandoned by his/her parents. It sends a clear message-that he/she is unlovable.

I had to get an abortion, and I had to take care of it quickly. I was moving soon. I wanted a clean slate and a fresh start.

Sharon, May 1971

After I came home from the hospital, Peter came to visit. He could see I was not doing well emotionally. He held the baby and was really quite good with her. He was much more natural than I had ever been. It made me really see him then, this gentle, good man. He started talking and didn't stop for a long time. I think he was trying to get my mind off the situation, and he needed to finally get something off his chest.

"I'm going to be graduating next week. I think we should get married."

I sat there listening.

"You're a good person, Sharon. I know it's been a bad year for you, but I've enjoyed the time we've spent together. Not only would it be helping you, but it would help me. My parents have been pressuring me to date and settle down, and I just haven't been interested in doing that until now. I want to start a family, and I have a career lined up. I know I can be a good husband to you."

"Okay," I said and shrugged my shoulders.

It was quite simple. After giving birth and trying to care for the baby, I had realized that my life was so different than what I had ever envisioned. In my young frame of mind, at seventeen years old, my life was over. I was angry at Mike and John. I was angry at my parents for making me have and keep the baby. But most of all, I was angry at myself. This was one thing I could do right-make it easier on them so they wouldn't have to keep this burden anymore.

Catherine

I took the subway to Marc's apartment. I didn't call first and didn't even consider the possibility that he might have company. He was there. He was getting ready to head out to shoot hoops with his brother. He was still the most handsome man I had ever laid eyes on. We would have made beautiful babies.

I didn't want anything from him. I knew there was no relationship to continue so I didn't spare his feelings when I blurted out, "I'm pregnant."

"Hhhhow do you know?"

"Because I took a test. Last night."

"Sometimes they're wrong, aren't they?"

"Maybe, but not this time. I feel it. I'm dreadfully tired. I've never missed. You didn't use anything, did you? I mean, we never discussed it."

"No, I didn't. What are you going to do?"

"What am *I* going to do? *I'm* not the only one involved here."

I was getting hysterical. This whole situation seemed unreal to me. I didn't even know this guy but he was irritating me. It must be nice to just scoff off responsibility because you're a guy!

"I'm sorry. That was stupid. What would you like to do? I'm sorry but I'm not ready to be a father."

"I want an abortion."

"Phew. I'm relieved. At least we agree. What can I do?"

"I need to find a doctor and it'll be done. I'll let you know when it's over. You don't have to do a damn thing." I turned and walked out the door.

Fucking men! Not only were they insensitive, but they were assholes! He got to just go on with his life while I had to go through the physical and emotional trauma of an abortion alone. I had enough on my plate right now.

Catherine

I found an obstetrician in Arlington and had to get an appointment to confirm the pregnancy and discuss options. That appointment took one and one-half weeks to get. They fit me in due to the move and because I was considering abortion. Normally, they didn't want to see you until you were eight weeks along.

In the meantime, Marc called and asked if he could take me to the appointment and pay for the abortion to ease his conscience. I agreed to it. I figured it was least he could do for getting me into this situation. Plus they wouldn't let me drive after the procedure.

We sat in the waiting area after they had drawn my blood in the lab downstairs. An hour later, the OBGYN called me into his office. He confirmed I was almost six weeks pregnant and would like to do an exam and discuss options.

"Wait a minute! I wasn't with you six weeks ago! This baby isn't even mine!" yelled Marc.

I almost choked. I was so embarrassed and looked to the doctor for help because I couldn't speak.

"I'm sorry I didn't explain more thoroughly. We date the pregnancy by going back to the first day of the last period, which was February 12th, according to our records. That would make it almost six weeks ago. The date of conception was probably 11-14 days after that which would make it in the range of the last week of February. Does that coincide with your recollection?"

"Yeah, sorry, I just wanted to make sure." Marc stammered.

How dare he accuse me of sleeping around? I haven't been with anyone in ages! I could kill him for the embarrassment he just put me through. I couldn't even look at him the rest of the morning as we spoke to pro-choice and pro-life counselors, a necessity prior to booking the appointment. They brought up financial and support groups to help raise the baby, adoption, etc.

"I would never give my baby up for adoption." I said fiercely. *So it can go through life like I have? Feeling unloved and unwanted?*

They even went on to say I would never sleep at night if I went through with this. I would never forgive myself. Feeling relieved that part was done, we booked the appointment for later in the week. I just wanted to get home and get away from Marc and the rest of the world.

Sharon

We broke the news to our parents over dinner the following evening. Peter was great by holding the baby for me and giving me a much-needed break emotionally and physically. Both sets of parents were shocked. Once we told them all the pros and that we did care for each other, they gradually gave their blessing. I thought my parents were the first to be relieved and accept the decision. Peter's parents respected our family enough, since they were good friends, to agree to the union. My belief was they were secretly relieved to see Peter show some interest in girls. At eighteen, he had never had a true girlfriend although he was very busy with school and sports. Both parents did know how well we got along and what good company we had been to each other.

It was settled. We started to plan the simple ceremony immediately. It was odd. I had imagined my wedding day to be special and something I couldn't wait for. I had pictured a big church wedding at a place where we finally had settled down.

All of our friends from all over the world would come. I would be in a big white dress with a train that flowed down the church aisle.

My husband would be handsome and someone with whom I was deeply in love -a man like my father with family ideals, who would shower me and our kids with love. I imagined the white picket fence and taking care of babies. But this? This wedding was the means to an end. It was an easy end to a bad chapter. However, the next chapter didn't look that much better.

Catherine

He picked me up as he had said he would. I told him I would rather go alone. I didn't need him to be there. He wouldn't be allowed in anyway; he'd have to wait in the waiting room.

We checked in, and he took care of the bill. They called my name, we stood, and he hugged me. I just stood there stiffly. Physical contact was what had gotten me in this mess. I didn't want him near me. The nurse had me change and lay down on the exam table with my feet up.

"You must hate your job," I said.

"Actually, it's very rewarding for the most part. This is the sad part."

The doctor came in and started prepping.

There was a picture on the ceiling of a field of butterflies. The nurse looked down at me and said, "Go ahead and squeeze my hand as hard as you need to. It's going to feel as if your insides are being ripped out." And it did. Tears ran down my face as I tried not to think of the pain, and what a terrible person I was to be doing this.

I thought of my mother and what she had gone through when she found out she was pregnant. I wondered if she had considered abortion. It wasn't legal in 1971, but I'm sure there were ways. It was then I decided I needed to know. Once I was settled back in Massachusetts, I would find her.

Catherine

After the abortion, life went on. The weird thing was I felt no remorse. I had some heavy cramping and had to go back for a shot because of my rare blood type but my body healed. My energy increased, and I finished out my time in DC. I packed what few belongings I had and was on my way.

I wondered, as I drove away, will every chapter in my life be like this: a learning experience with no true happiness. Was I destined to make bad choices and live with the consequences?

I drove 95 North and never looked back. I sang alone to the radio to keep my sanity.

Sharon

The wedding was planned for the next month. I must admit that I let both mothers take over the details. It gave them something else to focus on other than the unwanted birth. In retrospect, I thought it just gave me too much alone time with the baby. Something I didn't relish. One day when everyone was gone and Peter had started his new job, I had had it! The room was getting smaller, and her screams were getting louder.

"Shut up!" I screamed back. I was on my bed and staring angrily at the crib on the other side of the room. *I fed you and changed you. What else do you want from me?*

I could give this baby the necessities, but I could not love it. She was the reason I was so miserable. I didn't want to hold her and comfort her. I wanted my old life back.

I turned up the radio loudly to drown her out and eventually she cried herself to sleep. I relished the time to myself, dreading when I would have to care for her again, hoping someone else would come home to do it for me in the meantime.

Catherine

The shelter work was rewarding but hard. My realistic approach helped because we just couldn't save every animal. To think so would have led to fast burnout. I bonded with the animals in a way I never could with people. I instituted programs on pet placement and selection for the public. I organized fundraisers and networked, but mostly spent time with the animals. I was always up for fostering a new litter that had lost their mom and needed bottle feeding. My life revolved around my work. I loved it and couldn't wait to start each day. I had finally found my place in the world.

Through the shelter grapevine, I was referred to one of the large donors who needed a house and pet sitter on and off throughout the year. They had a separate "servant's quarter" that was vacant and needed their cats fed and watched over while they traveled often. The house was located at Quitnesset on Morris Island in Chatham. Morris Island used to be the land that connected

Monomoy Island to the mainland town of Chatham. During a storm in April 1958, Monomoy separated from Morris Island. Cars used to travel this way to get to Monomoy when it was inhabited. Only one cottage still stands today with a life –use lease by the U.S. Fish and Wildlife Service. There also stands a lighthouse that is no longer in use as of 1923 on South Monomoy.

Chatham is a quaint little fishing village with a vast history of ships which have wrecked trying to maneuver around Nantucket sound. It was said it was a place of rest and inner peace. Being there was as close as you could get to your own center. It seemed like the perfect place for me. I still wasn't healed.

The "servant's quarters" was a small cottage located south of the main house. The ocean was a stone's throw away, and you could feel and smell the breeze constantly. The house had two bedrooms, one bath, a kitchen with a three- season breakfast nook, and a living room with deck. It was rent free, but I had to be available year round to take care of the house, plants and cats while they are away. They trusted someone from the shelter and had required references from all previous landlords. I got their mail, checked up on the cleaning service, fed the cats, took them to the vet, and made sure heating and other housing necessities were working. This was in exchange for rent. It seemed simple, and I never felt taken advantage of. We became fast friends and always helped each other out.

Sharon, May 1971

"It's been almost two weeks, Sharon, and you haven't taken care of your baby. You need to help. You're the mother," My mom said accusingly.

"I don't want it. I never did. You and dad made me keep it. You deal with it."

"We have a post delivery appointment with the doctor today, and we'll discuss this with him."

We went as a family: My dad, mom and I. The baby went, also. We checked out fine physically. The baby was already over 10 lbs and loved to eat. I think my mom overfed her to make up for the lack of nurturing from me.

I told the doctor I couldn't do this. I told him I hated this baby. Every time I looked at her, I saw the rape. I saw the father- whomever that may be. I had finally told my parents the short version of what had happened in Rhode Island. I told them two boys surprised me in the shed, that they must have followed me home. I told them I was raped and had done nothing to provoke the attack. I begged them not to press charges. The reason I hadn't told them or the police was I was humiliated and didn't want the community to think less of us. Dirty laundry was not something to be aired.

They decided there was nothing we could do about it now. The proof of the rape was gone other than the fact that I had been pregnant. It would be too traumatic on the baby and me to go back and forth for the trial. But I knew it was mostly to save the family name. There was a solution now. Peter had stepped up to the plate. He was a martyr.

Catherine, Summer 1991

I could feel the dull ache spreading. It started under my right scapula through the back of my neck and settled right between the eyes. It was becoming a bad habit to knead there with my fingers. No matter how many visits to the chiropractor, I couldn't seem to shake this tension. I was sitting on my deck overlooking the ocean. There was a light breeze, and it was a warm night. I was sipping a chardonnay and contemplating my lack of sex when my best friend and neighbor came down the path.

Shane was carrying a bottle of wine, also, as if he had read my mind. We were like soul mates. We could finish each other's sentences and read each other's thoughts. I felt as if I've known him my whole life, not just months. The time we spent together was like déjà vu. There was a familiarity to it. With Shane, I was myself. I could be rotten to the core or an emotional wreck and he was never judgmental.

"Hey, Sweetness!" He stooped to kiss me on the lips, dropped a yellow rose in my lap, and went to get a glass. He pulled his chair in front of mine and my legs automatically went up to rest on his thighs.

"Careful. I haven't shaved. No reason to," I warned him. I poured him some wine and he started to massage my calves.

An outsider would think we were the sweetest couple, but it wasn't like that with us. He was just the best friend I had ever known. I loved him and couldn't imagine life without his charming wit or support.

"Hmm... that's good. Crisp," He commented on the wine. His smile at the end of a rotten day lit up the sky. He had short, cropped blond hair and amazing blue eyes. His glasses suit him and had always been a weak point for me in men. He was tall in height and when he hugged me, his blanket of security surrounded me.

"Have you written?" I asked. He was an amazing writer. Occasionally, he would send me a letter as a surprise treat. I cherished them. I couldn't wait until he finished his novel so I could read it in full.

"Well, I added to the fall of modern existentialism and what I consider to be the most influential philosophic moments of all time."

"Funny. Writer's block?"

He got up to put on Tracy Chapman. We listened to this album all the time. ... "*But you can say Baby. Baby, can I hold you tonight? Baby, if I tell you the right words, at the right time, would you be mine?"* Music was so important to me. At every point in my life, there had been music that fit that time. I could hear a song and it would take me back. I could stay here forever-just sitting with Shane, listening to the waves trying to drown out the music, smelling the salty air, and sipping chilled chardonnay. In one thought, I was thinking: *it doesn't get any better than this.* In the next, I was thinking: *You're still hiding.* Instead of investigating it any further, I asked, "Would you like more wine?"

Sharon

I awoke to the sound of crying. I laid in bed, not being able to move, not wanting to move. *Another day to dread.* The thought of making it through one more day like the last made death seem tempting. I had no enjoyment left in life. I stopped doing anything that I used to enjoy. Some days I didn't even bathe. I was numb. The heaviness that settled over me was stifling. I had no idea how or why I felt this way. Sometimes when I was cooking, I thought of how it would be if I slid the knife across my wrists. Or when I was riding in the car, it took every ounce of energy not to grab at the wheel and smash the car into a tree. I just wanted it all to end. Even the wedding plans that were hastily taking place could not motivate me.

I didn't think it was normal to feel hate for your own flesh and blood. But I did, I hated her. She was a constant reminder of my stupidity. Unlike other mothers who wanted to hold their children close, I could not wait until my mother took over and comforted her. I could not give her what she needed. I just wanted this over.

Suddenly, the thought of giving her away to someone, anyone, popped into my head. I could go back to my life, pretend this never happened. Maybe someone could love her.......

The solution was so crystal clear now. I couldn't believe I hadn't thought of it before. I packed up her diaper bag, put her in the stroller, and headed out across town. To everyone else we appeared to be taking a beautiful spring walk. Wasn't that what life's all about? Appearances?

Catherine

I was heading to work one morning. It was beautiful with a light ocean breeze. You could smell the sea faintly, and I had a desire to play hooky. Then guilt got the best of me, and I dutifully arrived at work. Apparently, my boss had hired a landscaper to mulch and plant the beds over the weekend, and the work really dressed up the shelter. They had planted a Japanese red maple in the corner bed with flowering perennials to the sides. There was even miniature silver iris which had always been a favorite of mine. The azalea and rhododendron were well-established. The hydrangea was a deep blue, almost purple, and I wondered if the old wife's tale was true. It was said that if you desire deeper color, put a rusty nail in the soil and the iron will turn the flower's color. Anyway, the whole design flowed nicely.

The crew appeared to be just finishing up. Unfortunately, the view from my window overlooked their work. I couldn't concentrate on anything but the tanned, muscular forms in front of me. Strong, hard-working, sweaty men have always appealed to me and it had been a long time since I had been with anyone. My hormones were getting the best of me. *Focus on work!* I kept telling myself, but my eyes couldn't leave him. He had the bluest eyes and a strong jaw line. He had an easy laugh and joked often with the other men. He was tall and thin with well-defined muscles that were more from hard work than working out. I had just given into my day dreaming when I noticed he was looking directly at me! I blushed and got up from my chair quickly and left the room. *You immature fool! Great first impression.* Maybe a cup of coffee would settle me. I visited with the other technicians while I drank. Shortly after, I headed back to the office, rounded the corner, and smashed right into him. I stumbled, and he caught me. What he didn't realize was, I stumbled more from his touch than the impact. His chest had been rock hard, and the smell of his sweat was intoxicating, and his voice......*Get a grip!*

Our eyes met again, and I mumbled, "Thanks...uhm, sorry."

"It was my pleasure. Good day." He left. I watched his truck and trailer pull away but noticed the name on the side first: Anthony's Seasonal Maintenance.

Catherine

My landlords were back for a week and as a homecoming celebration wanted to take me out to a nearby pub. They knew I had trouble meeting people and were not so subtle in their attempts to introduce me to the hot spots of the Cape. The Olde Inn at West Dennis appeared in the oldest atlas of Barnstable County, printed in 1879. At that time, Main street in West Dennis was known for the homes of its' affluent ship owners. The house of a shipmaster Obed Baker was just down the road, and other neighbors included well-known sea captains Peter Crowell and Uriah Fisk. The first owner of The Olde Inn was Captain Coleman Studley. The Studley's, a family of seafarers, were already long-time residents of Cape Cod. An ancestor, Benoni Studley, was known to have served under General George Washington during the siege of Boston. Another ancestor, Ansel Lothrup Studley, was badly wounded at the Battle of the Wilderness in 1864. He returned to West Dennis and sometime later died of his wounds.

The unconfirmed, yet persistent, sightings of a uniformed figure about the premises have sparked much speculation that the spirit of this Civil War hero still stood watch over The Olde Inn to this day.

We arrived at shortly after 9 o'clock, and the parking lot was packed. We were greeted at the door by the host, Kenny, whose Gaelic accent was still thick. As we entered the pub, I was transported to a quaint, dark, pub in Ireland. It was as if time were reversed, and I was in the old country. The barmaid and wait staff were all students who had come over seas to work, and you could hear the authenticity of their brogue. We found the last empty table against the dark wooden plank walls with dimly-lit lanterns and Gaelic sign postings. Even though it was early summer, it was rainy and raw out tonight so the fireplace was roaring. I ordered Guinness on tap and the Irish stew. I felt so at home the minute I walked in and could see why Bob and Jan liked it here. While we were waiting for our food, we were treated to a song sung by the host. When he appeared before the microphone, the entire bar went silent. There was obviously great respect for this man. He told us the song was a tale of a lonely man in Ireland who was met with great hardships. Before he started, he called up his great-nephew to sing with him. I almost choked on my beer as the landscaper from earlier in the week walked up. There was that smile again. He was obviously comfortable with himself the way he held himself and dared to sing to a crowd. The host, Kenny, would sing Gaelic while Anthony would sing the English version. What an incredible performance! The longing and sadness of the tale was so evident in their voices that even if we hadn't had the English version, we would have known it was a woeful song. Everyone there had tears in their eyes as they finished. If I heard that song everyday for the rest of my life, it would have the same effect on me.

We stood to applaud them, our eyes locked, and I saw him hesitate just slightly. He made his way to the bar while stopping to chat with people along the way. He wore a V-neck brown sweater with jeans that hung in all the right places. He wore his wallet in the left pocket which I thought odd, and one of his belt loops was torn. Not that I was looking.....

Moments later, he was standing at our table with a round of drinks "For the beautiful lady". *What a talker. That's the sign of a womanizer.*

Catherine

When I come to, it's quiet. How long have I been passed out? It's daylight now. Where is he? I pull myself up using the end table. It's a struggle and my whole body feels like a punching bag. What is that crackling noise? It sounds bad. It's coming from my chest. It's hard to breathe. I have to take very shallow breaths. If I try to breathe deep, it's painful. Like a knife through my heart. I try hard to avoid panic. The room is spinning and I can't seem to focus. I have to sit. I look around and see the apartment is in shambles. Last night was bad. I don't know exactly what I do that pushes his buttons but I'm constantly walking on eggshells. Our relationship is extremes. When it's good, it's great; when bad, it's becoming this. It was never like this. It somehow slowly developed over time. The fights became more heated. Eventually, it became a normal part of how we dealt with anger.

Looking around I concluded that he obviously left... left me for dead. He thinks so little of me. Not knowing what else to do, I start *cleaning up. If I remove the evidence, maybe it'll be like it never happened. I struggle to stay conscious but the pain evolves and I rest frequently. Out of sight, out of mind. But I can still feel his hands closing around my throat...*

"Aaaaaaaaaaaahhck!" I was awake now, covered in sweat, shaking, hyperventilating. I felt my neck, I still felt his hands there. I punched in the numbers on the phone.

"I'll be right there," he said without a hello, without needing to ask. Shane came in his boxers and a T-shirt. He turned on the overhead light above the stove, came to me and hugged me.

"Another nightmare, Dear Heart?"

I simply nodded.

"Were you able to wake yourself the way she taught you?" I nodded again.

"Your therapist said this would happen when you felt secure enough to deal with it. You still haven't even dealt with the anger." He took my hand and led me to the kitchen stool. He grabbed the pint from the cabinet and poured me a shot of Tequila. The chills I got from drinking that shot took precedence over the nightmare shakes.

We laid on the couch, my head in his lap, and watched David Letterman while he rubbed my back. The warmth in my belly was nothing compared to the warmth I got from being with Shane.

"I love you."

"I love you, too, Sweetness."

Sharon

Brightside was an old Renaissance-looking building behind iron gates. It looked like an old castle with beautiful gardens. I immediately felt hopeful here. It was run by the Sisters of St. Joseph. I had heard they ran an orphanage, and I blindly made my way through town to their doorstep. They were very kind to me and took an instant liking to my baby. As they oohed and ahhed, they asked, "What is her name?"

"I never officially baptized her." She wasn't mine to name because she wasn't mine to keep I had thought to myself.

I spent a good part of the afternoon there, praying with the Sisters and asking for the Lord's forgiveness. They counseled me and put me at peace.

When I left Brightside late that afternoon, I left empty handed with an empty heart. The relief I felt in that moment would become a constant guilt I would carry with me always. A huge weight had been lifted off my shoulders, and I realized I had taken the easy way out. I realized God and my parents would never forgive me. But most of all, I would never forgive myself; not for the act itself as much as for the joy I felt after giving her away.

It was late spring.... A time of Rebirth. As I walked, I concentrated on the sun in the sky and the birds singing. And I couldn't think of a more beautiful day.

Catherine

The surf was pounding the rocks today. It was high tide, but due to a coastal storm the waves were bigger than usual. It was deafening and I loved it. It blocked out my thoughts, which were particularly heavy today. The wind, the sound, the smell could almost make me forget. I could sit here for hours but only allowed myself to sneak a few moments. I thought if I stayed, I'd be hypnotized, a slave to the sea like the sailors to the Sirens in Greek mythology.

The moon would be full tomorrow but it was so bright tonight it could fool you. It was beautiful but I preferred the foggy mist of overcast days-the unknowing of what was out there. The possibilities were endless. I could hide in that dense air as I've been doing for the past three years. I was so lonely. I had friends or so they called themselves. Other than Shane, they were not the type I would go to with a problem. They were surface friends-friendships based on convenience. I had come to know the true colors of people early in life. I had high expectations and knew many would not meet them. Yet I wouldn't settle anymore. I didn't need to.

Sometimes I daydreamed I was a hermit and lived in a log cabin far away from every thing-no closeness to people, and no temptation. It would be better. At least if I weren't surrounded by so many people, I would have a true reason to be lonely.

Catherine

Shane just called, and I was meeting him today for a sunset picnic on the beach. I was throwing on my bathing suit and finishing the bruschetta. I saw he was already there, taking the kayak down to the shore.

"Hey."

"Hey, Sweetness," he stopped what he was doing and kissed me on the cheek. He would make someone a fabulous boyfriend someday.

"Do you want to kayak first?"

"Sure but we need to go before it gets dark. I hate the dark water. You don't know what is lurking down there." We got into his tandem boat and started paddling parallel to the shoreline.

"You know it's okay not to know." He mentioned absent-mindedly.

"What?"

"You seem to need to know everything ahead, have everything planned out. Things happen. Plans get screwed up. You adapt. Even you."

I was silent, paddling, controlling my breathing. So he continued with his philosophy.

"You made it into a career you love even though college was pulled out from under you; You were brave enough to make a move to a place where you didn't know anyone; You survived an abusive relationship. You've adapted, Catherine. No matter what, we're all programmed to keep going."

We kept going, in silence. The sun was at one end of the sky and the moon in another.

"It's too bad you're not happy." He added.

"I'm happy."

"Okay on the surface, maybe. But you don't let people in. You have these walls. Don't let that asshole keep you from ever having a relationship again. Sex in a relationship is even better, you know. Not as awkward, not as critical."

"Yeah, yeah, Mr. Relationship Expert."

"Stop putting me off. You need to face some things, get over it, and move on. You're stuck. You should address your mother and get this self-esteem thing put to rest and you should open up your heart to some lucky man. Hey, I'll volunteer for that or you can just use me for sex." I splashed him with my paddle. We laughed. It was so easy together.

Sharon

It was absolute madness at home when I arrived without the baby. My parents were unable to get her back after pleading with Brightside. I was the legal guardian, and I had signed her away and there were witnesses. There was nothing they could do. They had to move on with the wedding.

It took place at the town hall with our parents as witnesses. We had a small church reception and those invited were thrilled with my recovery from illness. I was still not sure how in a small town we were able to keep the baby a secret. I thought it was because I was so self-involved and home ridden that I had just become invisible.

At the wedding, my parents were the proud parents with transparent smiles. After the wedding, my parents stopped speaking to me. They felt betrayed and couldn't forgive me for letting go of their grandchild.

Peter and I got an apartment in Sunderland above a general store. It was beautiful out there with the rolling green valleys filled with cucumber and tobacco fields. The Connecticut River ran through it. Peter was the manager of one of the tobacco fields out there. It was hard work but only seasonal. I helped out in the store below to help with the rent.

When we got married, we didn't consummate the marriage. Peter thought I needed time to recover from the pregnancy. It had only been a month after all! I was more than happy for him to leave me alone. I wasn't looking forward to revisiting intercourse, although I assumed Peter would be more gentle. Time passed slowly; but we weren't in any hurry. We were just biding time.

Catherine

When we got back to the beach hours later, it was already clouding in. We had gone out near Monomoy and had seen the seals. They were amazing. It was too bad no one could live out there anymore. If I could go back in time, that was where I'd go. I'd be a sea captain's wife living on the rough, changing waters of Monomoy. Or maybe I'd be the captain myself.......

Shane interrupted my daydreaming.

"Would you like some wine? Tonight's choice is a California Pinot Noir."

"I would love some. I'll pour, you take care of the boat."

We laid on the blanket of our own deserted beach. We gingerly ate finger foods and sipped our wine.

"I heard back from some of my resumes I sent out. One was an editing position in a publishing company." Shane admitted.

"Wow. That's great! When will you know?"

"I fly out tomorrow morning. If I want it, it's mine. It's in Washington DC, ironically."

"I'm so happy for you! Call me as soon as you get back so I can hear all about it. This is the break you've been waiting for. You must be psyched."

"I would love the job but don't want to leave you."

"Shane, we'll always be friends. I knew when I met you that you wouldn't be here for long. I'll just have to find some other man to make me smile at the end of the day," I said coyly.

The sky was dark now with the beautiful moon hidden by clouds. Not a star in the sky.

"We should head up," I said regrettably. Just then it started raining. Not a light introduction either. The candles went out instantly. I started to get up to run.

"Wait," Shane grabbed my arm. "I know you. Let me know all of you. No strings attached. You know I'm leaving." He kissed me. It was so familiar. Like I had known this kiss before, from my imagination or another life, I don't know. But it awakened me. My body seemed to have shut down for so long, but now it was screaming for attention. His tongue was thick and took over my mouth. His taste was a mixture of rain and sea spray from our jaunt in the kayak. I couldn't feel the cold of the wind and rain. My body was on fire. All those nights of closeness, of him holding me, rubbing my legs, had worked up to this moment. I could smell his familiar smell, and I wanted to take it all in. He kissed me everywhere. He knew all my favorite places from all our graphic late night talks about sex. He made his way down to my soft folds and teased me achingly until I was begging for an end. He came up and plunged into me. We stayed there like that for a few moments, looking into each other's souls, just enjoying the unity. Knowing we had always been close, now there were no limits, no barriers. He moved in me slowly, building a rhythm that I met with no inhibitions. There was no shyness or newness. It was as if this was supposed to happen. The hard rain was matching our passion. It had built to a fiery crescendo and was about to erupt. We locked eyes and with no abash we came together. It was as if he went in and released my soul.

Sharon, 1972

Peter's parents started asking for grandchildren. The requests were tentative at first but then became more demanding. I thought they were relieved that their only son didn't have to raise a bastard child. However, they were looking forward to a legitimate grandchild.

Not many newlyweds went more than a year without creating a baby. It wasn't until over a year that Peter came home with a baby on his mind. This would be the first time we would have sex since our marriage vows were said. He asked me if I was feeling well enough and thought it was time for us to start a family. I knew his parents were pressuring him, and he had helped me, so I felt I owed him a child. He had never asked much of me. We were stable in our work and home. I honestly didn't think I could have given him a reason not to. He had been very patient with me thus far.

Peter and I had sex the very next night. It was awkward. We were both nervous and fumbling around. Right before he was about to enter me, he flipped me over and entered me from behind. I thought it was easier on both of us not to be facing each other; looking into one another's eyes. That would just add to the discomfort. It really wasn't as bad as I had expected. It was over before I knew it. He simply got up and left the house. I didn't know what I had done wrong. Peter came home late that night with whiskey on his breath, and before he passed out, he apologized for being so weak.

Catherine

The next day, Shane left. I didn't think much of what had happened yesterday. It was a normal act in our deep friendship. We had shared so much about ourselves that it seemed only natural for us to make love. It also didn't change anything. We both knew it wouldn't go anywhere at this point in our lives.

What I did think about was our conversation. I felt I was lucky enough to have someone in my life that could tell me the truth even if it was not flattering. The fact that Shane was insinuating that I used my adoption as a crutch bothered me. He was right. I also had been using the abuse as a crutch. No, I didn't come right out and tell people. But in my mind, it was what I went back to. It defined me. *Poor me, the one that no one wanted.* I was just discarded by everyone because I was not loveable. It set the stage for my self image everyday. I kept everyone at arms' length- everyone but Shane. It helped keep me safe from people. I even avoided people by working with animals.

I spent the day in deep thought. I cleaned my house. I paid bills. I went for a run. I realized there was still that question in the back of my mind: Who was I really? Was I the product of environment or hereditary? Where did I get my smile? Which parent did I take after? I had always hoped for answers. Now I felt as if was the time in my life to get the answers and be done with it. I remembered growing up. Every birthday was spent hoping, waiting, for a call. Dreaming my birth mother would call to wish me a happy birthday, filling in all the missing pieces, I could finally be complete. It never happened. She never called. She probably never gave me a second thought. To this day, I still don't celebrate my birthday. Maybe it was time to stop feeling sorry for myself and do something about it.

I called a contact that I had made at work while adopting out a Great Pyrenees mix. He had done some work with the head of someone at TRY Adoption Resource Services. He would call the president and call me back with details of what I needed to do to get the ball rolling.

Sharon, 1973

Steve was born exactly nine months and eight days after Peter and I had consummated the marriage. When I told him that I was pregnant, he was so happy and relieved. He hadn't touched me since except for the occasional kiss on the forehead. I think he was happy it took the first time so he didn't have to relive the experience again. I wondered what I had done wrong and tried extra hard to make everything just right for him.

Steve was an easy baby. I didn't want to put him down. Peter doted on him and was very proud. I felt I had aged greatly in the last couple years and since living on our own, I felt more mature and able to handle an infant. I stopped working at the store and spent all my time caring for him. We had to move to a bigger apartment for the extra bedroom. Life was progressing as planned and I was enjoying mother hood. I had sworn to myself that I would feel differently about this baby than I had about the other. I thought of her everyday and never forgave myself for leaving her.

When I looked at Steve, I saw so much promise. I could do things right by him. It was as if I was given a clean slate.

Catherine

I left the support group meeting feeling dumfounded. Those people didn't know what they were talking about! Attending a meeting was one of the requirements in order to have a search done of my birthparents. The birth mothers and children who were given up to adoption told stories of segregation, reunions gone bad, and broken expectations.

One woman just drove to the house and watched her child playing in its new yard and was beside herself with guilt even though the child seemed so happy. Another woman didn't ever want to know the outcome of her child, it was too painful. Other women met their children and felt estranged with no connection to them.

That was not me. I had always known when my birth mother and I met we would instantly be best friends. We were just like one another. She would finish my sentences for me and be full of motherly wisdom. I would be the highlight of her life.

"Catherine." My thoughts were interrupted by Ann, the head of the institution, who was catching up to me at my car.

"Thank you for coming. I hope you found the meeting useful. It's to give you insight into all the possibilities of a meeting with your birth parents. Please consider them all. Can you give me all the information you have of your birth?"

"I was born at Westover AFB in Chicopee, Massachusetts on May 7, 1971. The hospital portion of the base closed down nine years after I was born and the records were transferred to the town hall. That's it."

"Okay. I will have an answer for you in two weeks."

That's it? $500 and two weeks and I've been spending all this mental energy on this?

I had read every adoption book out there. Records are sealed. She must have connections!

I didn't know if I could stand the wait, but I had already waited for twenty one years.

It was still early and I wasn't tired yet. I decided to stop for a drink and a bite to eat on my way home. Cooking for one wasn't exactly something to look forward to and Shane was away this week. I could use some friendly conversation. At least that was what I told myself as I drove into the lot of The Olde Inn.

I sat at the bar. It was a Thursday night and not too crowded. Although I didn't want to admit it, I was disappointed he wasn't there. Something about him had stayed with me, and I thought of him often. I was just finishing my chowder and Smithwicks when a voice caused me to look up.

"How about another one? On me, if I can join you." I looked to each side. "Sorry, no bar stools available." I was playing along, flirting with *the talker* from my work's landscape job.

He poured a couple of pints and said to follow. He showed me to the back dining area that was separate from the bar and the noise. We sat across from each other.

"I'm Anthony. It's nice to finally meet you." We spoke for a while about the work he had done at the shelter and the history of the bar. He was an Italian adopted by this Irish family. The brother of his parents owned the bar and it was like a second home for him to help out and visit his cousins and aunt and uncle. His parents were back in Ireland, and he was close to his relatives. He was also a twin. His sister, Andrea, lived nearby off cape.

It was getting late. "I need to get going. Thanks for the beer and conversation," I said as I stood, not wanting to leave him. I could stare into his blue-green eyes forever.

"I'd love to take you out. Will you go out with me?"

I hesitated. After my emotionally-draining night I had begun to realize that even seemingly trivial events in our life had consequences-that all of our events in life led to something. Was it fate? Was *this* fate? Why had I come here? After dealing with the adoption meeting and then to find out Anthony was also adopted was too coincidental. We had just hit the tip of the iceberg, and I wanted to know more about him. "Sure," I said before I realized it. When he smiled, his eyes lit up even more and I noticed the laugh lines around his eyes. He surprised me when he said, "How about tomorrow night?"

Catherine

The thought of my date that night had me sidetracked all day. I was so looking forward to seeing him. I left work and went home to shave and do my nails. I was normally not a vain person, but I wanted to look my best tonight. I threw in Sinatra and sang in the shower to "Fly Me to the Moon".

I chose a silk tank in a cognac brown and some comfortable capri's. It was nice but not overkill. I even paid attention to detail when it came to my underwear and wore a camisole and thong to match.

He picked me up at 8:00 on his Heritage Softail Harley Davison motorcycle. What did I expect? We rode to the Chatham Bars Inn. It was an amazing oceanfront resort. They had a restaurant and bar inside the hotel and across the street at the pool area, they had a beach bar restaurant and tables on the sand. They had a band starting later, but right now it was quiet for good conversation.

We went to the outside bar and had wine. I asked him about his birth parents and if he'd ever met them. His sister's boyfriend was a policeman and had looked up information for them. He went to look up his father and found he had passed away six months prior from Alzheimer's. I told him about my move and my search for my birth mother. He encouraged me to find them before it was too late, like his situation.

After dinner, we walked the beach down by the cabanas. You could see the boats and the fish pier lit up and the truck campers on Nauset. It was a warm night, and I was relaxed. Usually my guard was up around men. I didn't know if it was the wine or ocean air, but whatever it was, was putting me at ease.

It was low tide, and the water was quiet. Occasionally, I could hear a splash in the harbor. Anthony smelled of nutmeg and looked even better. He was such a gentleman. He held doors for me and treated me like a lady. All I wanted was to feel his lips on mine, to nuzzle my face in his neck, to take in the warmth of him. His voice interrupted my thoughts.

"Did you know that Chatham is locally known as "The First Stop of the East Wind"?" I shook my head no.

"It's always been my favorite town. It's also one of the Cape's oldest towns. The first time I explored it I ended up on Moon-cusser's Lane and found that the road ends abruptly at the water. I felt a connection and hoped no matter what road I took in life, I would end up at the water also." I just looked at him and marveled. Who knew I would meet this amazing man with so many layers? I was glad I hadn't stopped at my first impression of him.

The ride home was too quick. He walked me to my door. He stood close to me, too close. My head was whirling. I knew before his lips touched mine that this would be life-altering. It was as if we melted into one as he looked into my eyes, and I knew. My knees were weak, and I leaned against the door for support. It was like a roller coaster ride- the anticipation of the climb and then the drop-the fall takes your breath away. His need, the hunger we felt, it was all there in his eyes. He came closer and hesitated, teasingly, until I couldn't wait anymore. Finally, his hands cupped my face ever so gently, and I felt his lips on mine. His taste was so sweet and intoxicating. His tongue was shy at first, exploring. As his confidence and our desire built, it became more demanding. Every nerve was heightened, and my skin was tingling beneath his touch. There was warmth spreading through out my body, I was lost to all but him. At this moment, nothing else mattered, we were in prefect rhythm, our tongues, our breathing, our hearts, and I knew in this instant, I didn't want to be loved by anyone but Anthony. It was consuming me and I would never give this feeling up. It was exactly what I needed, what I had been searching for my whole life.

Catherine

Shane pulled up in his old, beat up station wagon. "Come ride with me, Dear Heart."

I had today off and wasn't up to much anyway. He had gotten in late last night from his interview.

"It must have gone well. You've been away a while."

"It was incredible. Want to come?"

"Like the last time or to DC?" I joked.

"Anything your heart desires."

We caught up on everything that had happened in the last week. Well, almost everything. I was unsure how to handle the relationship I was hoping to start with Anthony and Shane and my rendezvous on the beach. We drove with the windows down, listening to the radio. We ended up at Nauset beach. We watched the seals ride the waves with the surfers. We held hands, and it was dusk. I felt the mist of the cool ocean on my face. I could smell its' sweetness. This was my favorite time of day and I wished I could freeze time. I knew things would never stay the same, and I didn't want to give up Shane. I also knew we were outgrowing each other: he had his job and big move coming and I had my unknown future……my gut told me Anthony might have a part in that.

Shane left the next month for DC. It was the first time I had felt a drift between us. It was as if we had to distance ourselves in order to deal with the fact that he was leaving. It was the only way. We spent time together but I missed our late night talks and the affection. It just didn't seem right, although harmless to us, while I was dating Anthony. The last time I saw him, he kissed me goodbye. He kissed my eyes that were overflowing with tears, he kissed my forehead, my lips. The last thing he said to me was, "I love you, Sweetness."

I went inside, feeling more alone than at any other time in my life. Knowing me so well, knowing exactly what I needed, he had left his favorite sea foam green sweater on my kitchen table with a note.

> There's a picture of us at the beach, me in my sweater and you in your bathing suit. You're always so warm! I know you're touching my sweater right now, smelling it, holding it.
>
> I think you would say it was a mistake, that all that happened did. I guess I would agree but I so desperately want to say it wasn't. No fooling myself now.
>
> There's a song and as I drive away from you I'm listening to the lyrics:

"Did you find the time
to keep us both in mind;
did you wander far from me?
..wander far from you?
And I like your face...
But I can't anymore."
Why did it have to change?
Even with that unanswerable question, I don't
think you can exonerate everyone for your
problems, especially me. You try to carry the
weight of the world and it's impossible.

I don't regret any of the time we spent and
would not change anything that happened.
Although in the end, we may have been wrong,
please do not look back at the short time we
spent together in anger, disgust, or
disappointment. Just remember it as an attempt
for the two of us to find our own little world
where we could escape and try to find
happiness there. I believe that there is a place
where you and I could be happy — I truly
believe that to be true. And with all your
cynicism, I know you feel there is a place and
time when you will be happy.

Shane

Thinking of it now made my heart ache. We were as close as two people could be. For most, the relationship turns sour over time and it's decided that it's over. For us, we ended on the best part, on the best terms. It was harder. Sometimes when I thought of paths not taken, I thought of Shane and what might have been.

Catherine

The call came two weeks to the day.

"Catherine, your name was listed as Jane Doe with the birth date of May 7, 1971. You were born at Westover AFB to a Sharon Dent. Last known address 27 Birch Lane, Palmer, MA. DOB 3-4-54. She married a Peter Szaban. Half-brother – Steve, also of Palmer. He was born in 1972. You also have a half-sister. Good luck to you."

I was shaking, staring at the information I had written down. All these years, the unknowing…. my mother……my mind was whirling.

I put in a call to Anthony to see if he would mind asking the policeman he had used to look up this information in the police database. It only took hours for me to have the information. Palmer was the last address in the RMV records for both my mother and brother.

Anthony's landscape business was in its' prime, and our time together was limited. Although he offered to help, I felt this was something very private and wanted to do this myself. I took a few days off and decided to head to western Massachusetts.

I had never been to the western side of the Quabbin Reservoir. I was able to find Birch Lane, but there was no such number as had been given to me. I decided to try my brother's address, also in Palmer. He lived in an apartment building. I had no idea what I would say, but I went to apartment B and knocked. No one answered. I tried the door. Locked. I was so close finally and striking out! Feeling a little desperate, I looked twice at the open, overflowing garbage bag outside his door.

Impulsively, I started picking through his garbage. I looked at overdue utility bills. I found an unpaid telephone bill. There were two numbers he called often, one in Enfield, CT and one in Shrewsbury, MA. The next stop was the local high school. I went to the office and said I was the daughter of Sharon Dent and needed a copy of her transcript. She had asked me to get it for her. They gave it to me. No questions asked. Is this legal? I wondered.

I drove by the house she had lived in on Squire Street. I went to the door and asked for Sharon. The little old woman who answered said there was no one there by that name, and she had lived there for 10 years at least. I passed the town hall while looking for a hotel for the night. I pulled a sharp right and went in to get a copy of the marriage certificate. She was married shortly after I was born. Was he my father? I paid $5.00 and walked out with a copy of my mother's history. *My mother* – I was still having a hard time believing this.

The Enfield number turned out to be Chess King at the Enfield Mall. When I called, I asked for Steve Szaban, and they went to get him. I hung up. Okay, that's where he works. The second number was a residence. A woman answered, but I hung up. *Was it she?* The anticipation and excitement kept me awake all night. I charted a route to get to Enfield for the next day.

I awoke full of hope. The possibility of finally knowing something about me was unnerving. Was I a good baby? How was I conceived? Whom did I look like?

I was going to find out all the answers.

I waited until noon when the mall would open since it was Sunday. I walked by the store three times before I went in. I pretended to look at the men's clothing, while checking out the sales people. I was approached by a young man who looked like a young version of Don Ho. He was of a large build, slightly overweight, dark skin, and definitely exotic looking. His name tag said Steve. I felt a rush of emotion, mixed with jealousy that he had a life with our mother while I had dreamed of it. Anticipation kept me from being politically correct. I blurted out, "Steve…. Are you Steve Szaban?" When he said yes, I said, "I'm your half-sister and your mother is my mother." He was definitely in shock and not too happy with my forthrightness. He argued that it couldn't be true. I could tell he didn't believe me, but I convinced him to ask his mother and gave him my name and number. I asked if he could ask her to call me. The ball was in her court.

Not knowing what the future held, I headed for home.

Sharon, 1991

"*What*?!" My mind was careening.

"A young woman came in today and introduced herself as your long-lost daughter. Mom, is it true?"

"I .....ohmigod. She's here? In Massachusetts?"

"Yeah. Mom, what's going on?"

"Steve, I can't discuss this with you right now."

"I told her I didn't believe her, but she knew a lot about us."

"Steve, honey, what did she look like?"

"She looked like Donna. She could pass for my sister."

There was a lump in my throat, and I could all but mumble a goodbye to my son.

All these years I had tried to put this behind me. My marriage to Peter had not worked out. We had both harbored each other's secrets for ten years. He had confessed to me after the birth of our second child that he was different. He wasn't attracted to women. He hated himself for it. We did love each other, but it was more like friends or roommates. We really had tried to be husband and wife sexually. On both accounts, I got pregnant. I didn't know if that whole situation prepared me or if it was the uneventful way that they were conceived, but I loved my children.

I had to admit that I've often wondered-all these years of not knowing. Not being sure if I wanted to know where she ended up. Looking at every girl who passed me on the street with dark hair, wondering if it was she. She had a head of black hair when she was born! I was so young. I didn't understand her innocence in all this and had blamed her for my mistakes.

How did she find us? Not that we've been hiding, but aren't adoption files sealed? It's been twenty-one years! Does she want to meet me? Does she hate me? What is she like? Where is she living? It must be close if she just showed up at Steve's work to talk to him.

The vivid memories of the rape I had blocked out so many years ago came rushing back. I couldn't relive this. How was I going to explain this to my children? At least I was truthful with one person.

Catherine

Anthony and I were spending every spare second of time together. He continued to surprise me with his thoughtfulness. He was always bringing me flowers and opening the door for me. He treated me like a princess. Although I had promised myself to take it slowly and steadily, I couldn't help but want more.

Soon he was spending the night, and little by little his personal items showed up: a toothbrush, CDs, his brand of beer, an extra set of clothes. We were opening up to each other like petals of a flower in the morning. Every thing was fresh and beautiful. I couldn't wait to wake up each day next to him.

At our six month anniversary, he arranged a romantic overnight at a local bed and breakfast. At dinner, we exchanged cards. We were surprised when we opened them to find we had bought the exact same cards for each other. The first line was "I loved you even before we met, because I have dreamed of you my whole life…"

Back at the room, he had candles lit everywhere. There was a big box wrapped with a bow on the feather bed and wine chilling in front of the fireplace. The Victoria Secret lingerie he had bought me fit perfectly. We sipped the wine and listened to a CD he had made just for me. I was overwhelmed with feelings. He made sweet love to me. That was, until I opened my eyes and couldn't see.

"Anthony, something's burning." I murmured.

"Oh yeah, baby, we're burning up." He wasn't paying attention to what I was saying but to the task at hand.

"No! The room is on fire!" I screamed. We jumped up and saw the feather pillow had hit a candle when it fell off the bed.

The pillow was engulfed in flames, and the rug was getting smoldered, also. He grabbed the pillow, threw it out the French doors and into the gardens below. Meanwhile, I was jumping up and down naked near the smoke detector, fanning it with the other pillow. All I could picture was the alarm going off and everyone running out of their rooms to see us jumping around naked.

He was the most romantic, amazing man I knew. Sometimes when we made love, I felt as if he were trying to break down my walls, but he could never get close enough. I think that's what finally pushed him away.

Sharon

"Steve, Donna, when I was younger, before I was married to your father, I was raped and gave the child up for adoption. I'm sorry I haven't told you, but it was a very difficult time for me. The girl in the store could very well have been she."

"But she's almost two years older than I. Couldn't you have kept her?"

"Mentally, I wasn't prepared to handle and raise a baby. Those two years were spent growing up, getting married. It was a big dose of reality."

"Don't cry, Mom." Donna was getting apprehensive.

"I don't want to relive my mistake and now it's here presenting itself. After I had the two of you, I couldn't imagine giving up a baby. I feel guilty about it constantly. How can she ever forgive me?" Bill grabbed my hand to give me support.

Bill was my boyfriend, the one man I had ever loved. After about 15 years together, Peter finally met someone with whom he could share his homosexuality, and he fell madly in love with him. It was his chance at happiness. Our marriage had served its purpose, and we were older and less vulnerable. It was an amicable split. I got a waitressing job to help support us and met Bill there. He was the one person I could talk to. He listened and expected nothing from me.

"Well she wants to meet you. She gave me her phone number to give to you." Steve said. My heart stopped. The ball was in my court. I took the piece of paper and got up.

"I need to lie down."

Catherine

It felt as if I were holding my breath for her to call. I needed to get out. It hadn't been long since I had met Steve but it felt like eternity. I was helping with another animal fundraiser so that helped some. We held a fair on the grounds outside the shelter. It was a gorgeous day. Money was flowing, and we met our goal. I was walking out near the end of the day to give the final tally. We had many booths set up with everyone donating a percentage of their day's income. I turned at the sound of a woman's voice, "Come. Let me read your future. The cards are calling you." I hesitated. I had never had my cards read before, but my life was hanging by a thread right now. What the hell.....

"This is where you've been. This is your present. This is where you are heading." She pointed as she laid the cards out in a pattern. It was a strong reading with many Major Arcana cards.

"Your past has been difficult, but it has made you strong. Here is the Hermit. A leader who draws upon internal wisdom and life's experience. The Lovers card indicates that you are in a period of making important choices about relationships in your life. The Hierophant represents the learning and teaching that is experienced in life's challenges that require us to trust our faith. The five of Disks – in the next five weeks or five months, you have the opportunity to release worry. Worry is an interesting state of consciousness because it takes us to the future and it takes us to the past, and totally avoids the present. Stop living in the what-ifs and if-onlys.

Your present is also your future. You will be married at 23. You have already met your future. It will not be an easy road, but you will get there in the end. You care for others. You will continue to care and take care of others as a career, but I don't see it within the human industry.

You will have three children. You will die at the age of 86."

It was a little unsettling...hearing all that. I worked with animals, but it would have been easy to figure that out. Married? I hadn't been in a serious relationship to consider it. However, I knew I would never have children. I had no desire to go through that. I have never been around kids but hadn't been impressed by those I'd seen. Kids-not me, not ever!

After the day fundraiser, a group of us from the shelter went out for drinks. I didn't want to go home to wait anxiously by the phone. The margaritas were flowing that night. I was slightly drunk and very tired. Before I went to bed, I checked the answering machine. There was a message from Anthony saying he was sorry but extremely busy. Could we have breakfast? Call in the morning when I woke. Message two was a shocker:

"Hi. This is your mom calling. I'll try you again another time." *That's it?!* I listened to her voice over and over again. I fell asleep on the couch hugging Shane's sweater with tears running down my cheeks.

Catherine

I waited …unsure of what to do with the message. It was as if my whole life lay in limbo.

All those birthdays, all those holidays, I waited and prayed for her to call me or want me or think of me. After so long, I realized if your own mother didn't want you, no one would.

Was there a connection? Did I sound like her? Should I call back? And then the anger rose … How dare she? She had abandoned me! What kind of monster could do something like that? In the back of my mind, I tried to fall back on the safe mode of "I hate her" and "How could she do this to me?" but curiosity got the best of me and I eventually called her back.

"Hello, Sharon. This is Catherine, your daughter….."

Catherine

We agreed to meet at a neutral restaurant that would be a mid-point for both of us. I waited impatiently outside for her. *Okay. I need to stop pacing!! She is going to be here any minute!* I was wondering if I should have changed. Was I too casual? But I didn't want to appear over anxious- even though I was. The woman that I have found out to be my birth mother was about to pull up, and I'm freaking out. A car pulled up. Nope, not her, I would feel it. I've known all my life that we were like two peas in a pod…so alike that we'll never be apart again. A few minutes later a black Buick pulled around the side of the building.

I wasn't clear on the license plate, but that could be that I couldn't get past the fuzzy dice hanging from the mirror. Although there were two people in the vehicle, I only focused on one. Then I saw her. She was not as I had imagined. She was a heavy set woman with jet black hair. She had a prominent Hawaiian white streak in her part. She wore too much make up;

I had always used minimal makeup. I had always imagined an older me. I didn't think we looked at all alike. In the split second that it took for her to slow down and then drive past, I was able to take it all in.

I saw my life go by. I saw my hopes and dreams go by and in one instance drowned. I couldn't even explain how I felt from the rush of all those years, but instinctively ran inside for the bathroom. It didn't matter any way. I knew she wasn't going to stop. There really wasn't a connection there. Her curiosity was satisfied.

When I got home, I called Anthony and couldn't reach him. I was so disappointed. Being adopted, he was the only one who could have understood what I was going through. I needed to feel his arms around me and hear him tell me everything would be all right.

He had been so busy with work lately, and his parents were coming into town. We had just celebrated our six month anniversary, but I was feeling out of the loop. He hadn't once mentioned introducing me to his parents. I knew he had always brought girlfriends home for his parents' approval and for some reason; I had a feeling that he didn't want me to meet them. In every aspect tonight, I was feeling discarded.

Sharon

I saw her immediately. I couldn't believe the resemblance to myself when I was young. It was shocking. Only 17 years between us, but I was showing the strains of my life. The guilt I had lived with had taken a toll, and I had let myself go. I was overweight and hid behind a mask of makeup. I thought if I wasn't attractive, I wouldn't attract other men, and then I wouldn't get into the same position I had been in years ago. Call me weak, but when I saw her, it all came back and I couldn't face it. I just couldn't go through with meeting her. *She was so beautiful and she had her whole life ahead of her.* I was resentful. My life had been a disaster. Maybe the only thing I ever did right was giving her away......

"Bill, I changed my mind. Take me home. Please take me home now!" Once home, I locked myself in my room and gave in to my tears and my grief. What had we hoped to gain by meeting? I was never good with confrontations to begin with. I couldn't make up for lost years. Why couldn't she leave well enough alone?

Catherine

I was still wounded by my non-meeting with my birth mother. To top it off, I was hearing from Anthony less and less. Not that he had any obligation to call. After all, we hadn't been dating that long. Maybe it was a summer fling. Maybe I was making this more of a relationship than he was. We hadn't actually discussed it. It was just that every time we were together was like magic, and I never wanted it to end. I also didn't want to appear too needy or too demanding. He was probably too busy with his business, and we had never discussed dating each other exclusively. In fact, I bet he had a whole slew full of wanton women. He was so hard to read. He seemed so easy to fall in love and had jumped right in head first from what I gathered from our conversations regarding past relationships. Why was he holding me at bay? I was used to men being interested and making no question about it. It has been several months, and I knew I was also the first girl he hadn't brought home. This concerned me.

Not because I was anxious to go through the meeting the parents thing, but because for the first time in my life, I was thinking in terms of forever.

Catherine

Anthony and I argued at the beginning of the weekend. He had gone away with his parents for the weekend, and we hadn't spoken since. I knew he would be home today and we had plans for a late dinner. I spent last night with my stomach churning. I've always had this sixth sense about me. I knew when something bad was going to happen. My gut was telling me he was with another woman.

No, I was not the jealous type. Either someone wanted to be with you or they didn't. There was a lot of temptation out there. But there was something to be said about someone who was your soul mate: the one who made you weak in the knees, the one who stimulated you mentally and physically, the one you'd rather die than live without. When you had someone so powerful in your life, it made the temptations less tempting. It gave you peace. There was clarity in your life for once. I was so sure Anthony was all that. Without seeing him, or speaking to him, I realized in my gut that he was not the perfect statue that I've been putting on a pedestal. He was human, he had temptations and there would never be one person to fill another's needs.

I wouldn't be as stupid as I once was. I didn't need him. I had myself and that was all there will ever be. I was angry and wanted to lash out at the world.

Sharon

The phone rang.

I was still feeling a deep depression from the almost meeting last week. I hadn't been to work and hadn't been out of bed much either. I just laid there numb. Not even Bill or my kids could seem to pull me out of this fog. I just didn't feel anything but this mind-blowing numbness. I had nothing left in me.

The phone was ringing and the answering machine finally picked up. It was Catherine.

"Sharon, are you there? I saw you at the restaurant. It's great to know you can't take responsibility for your actions – even 20 years later!" She hung up. This was for the better.

Bill kept asking if there was anything he could do. As the weeks turned into months, he became increasingly nervous. I lost my job, became a recluse, and even stopped returning the kids' phone calls. I wanted to give up. I had tried to create a happy façade, but I just couldn't live a lie anymore.

My family was very worried.

Catherine

"I know," I accused.

"What?"

"I know. Did she fuck you as well as I do?"

"You're crazy! What are you talking about?"

"Don't treat me like an idiot, Anthony. I want you to leave. If you want to screw around, go ahead, but not while you're with me."

"I went to see my parents...they're back from Europe. It was a big family reunion and you're freaking out over it." I could feel the white fury taking over. I needed air. I needed to calm down. It was as if everything is closing in.....I couldn't breathe.....

"TALK TO ME!" he yelled. All I knew is I couldn't handle this. I was angry. It was as if years of fear and pent up anger were surfacing and I was drowning in it. I needed to get out- to get away from this situation. I tried to leave.

Anthony grabbed my arm. "We need to talk about this. You always run away! Tell me what you are talking about!" Panic took over. He was yelling. He was in my face. He was all Italian, talking with his hands and all I could see was his controlling me and forcing me to stay. I totally lost it. I pushed him away and ran outside. He caught up with me as I was about to get into the car. He grabbed my keys.

"We need to talk about this. You need to chill. You're hysterical."

"GET OUT!!!!! GET OUT OF HERE!!! I HATE YOU. I FUCKING HATE YOU. HOW DARE YOU? YOU THINK I DON'T FUCKING KNOW? HERE.....GO TO HER."

I threw the card at him-the card I had found on his windshield after my morning run. She had been there-at my house. She had the cocky nerve to leave it for him in *my* yard. She even conveniently left it unsealed. I had read it:

Anthony,
Thank you for a wonderful weekend visiting your family. It is always nice to see them. You are very sweet. I especially liked our romantic walk on the beach. Let's do it again soon.
Love,
Jennie

He was apparently shocked. He simply got into his truck and said, "We'll talk later." Just like that. Just like I'm supposed to deal with it and like it. Just like I didn't matter. Just like things would be fine once I accepted his infidelities. I was at my boiling point. I had been made a fool of before, and I wasn't about to go through that again. Before he put the truck into drive, I jumped into the bed of his truck and grabbed his shovel. He was just starting to drive out the driveway, and I stood and started tapping his rear window with the shovel.

"Does your truck mean anything to you? How would you like to feel broken? How about I screw you over?" I was screaming and crying hysterically. It was as if I had no control. My anger was released, and there was no end to it. He slammed on his brakes, and I fell forward.

"Get out of my truck or I will call the police. You need to calm down." I could tell he was serious, and the thought of police hunting me down must have gotten through the fog. I got down, and he spun out and drove away. I made it three steps before I dropped and gave in to the sobs that had been stored up for years.

Sharon

I had a weakness. I couldn't seem to ask forgiveness from God, from Catherine, or from myself.

This depression was multiplying like cancerous cells and eating away at my mind. I couldn't seem to dig myself out of this. There seemed to be only one way to control an uncontrollable situation.

I started to contemplate suicide. I began getting my affairs in order. I just couldn't leave Bill with all these loose ends. It must be the Catholic guilt that resonated with me.

I spent years thinking I was better off without her, Catherine, but now I realized it was she who was better off. Perhaps she will find herself when I am not this presence that is constantly oppressing her.

Thank God for Steve and Donna. I needed to believe in something, to know that at least one part of my life mattered. Wasn't that what we all wanted to know-we made a difference? To know we've left the world a better place?

What was it like? This implausible theory of death? I often wondered if it was like sleeping. Then sometimes I pictured my spirit up in the evening sky and I could see myself outside of my body, but I can't seem to fathom death itself. I couldn't say I was not scared. It was the fear of the unknown that made me hesitate.

Just then Bill came home and slapped the mail on the bed. "What the hell is this?"

It was a copy of my last will and testament, recently updated.

Catherine

First I was angry. Then I was depressed. Then I was second guessing myself. My anger scared me and I was finally starting to look at it. I thought my madness was brought out or triggered by Glenn. Now I knew the anger remained, even when he wasn't here.

I called a hot line for abusive women. It was the first time I used that label on myself. I had seen a therapist for a short time when I started having nightmares, but she was a general therapist. They put me in touch with a therapist who specialized in post abuse traumatic disorder. I nervously met her on a Monday. I was really doubting how this would help me at all. That part of my life was over. I didn't even feel as if it happened to the same person. By the time of the appointment, I figured it couldn't hurt to try. What we found was I needed to finally deal with what had happened to me and I needed anger management. Over time, we perfected how to stop the nightmares and how to deal with confrontations without running or panicking.

I needed to move on. The opportunity to do this presented itself during one of my work fundraisers. It was a black tie dinner benefit. I busied myself by looking for the perfect dress. After much expended energy, I found a gorgeous floor length black velvet gown that was lined with a silver silk sash. It was beautiful. I needed to feel good about something since Anthony and my breakup.

I was introduced to an older gentleman named Jeff. He was very handsome with salt and pepper hair, extremely attentive and very rich. He smelled of husky cologne and wore a tux made in London. We danced. We flirted. He wanted to fly me to Spain.

Some attention and compliments were just what I needed after my humiliating spell with Anthony. My self confidence was at an all-time low, and I was reveling in his adoration.

We drank champagne with strawberries. We ate caviar. I could get used to the high life. He asked for my number. I gave it to him with some hesitation. Was I ready?

Sharon, 1993

Bill and I had finally married to make our relationship official. We moved from the condo to a small house. I thought he was trying to keep me busy so I wouldn't sink back into a depression.

Donna was busy in her junior year of high school and sending out applications to colleges. Our life had taken a smooth rhythm and I was trying to enjoy my life as much as I could. When my family threatened to commit me for round the clock care and therapy, I knew I needed to pretend I was better. I found a job at a dry cleaning company. It wasn't something that I loved, but it was a job and I hadn't had ambition to do anything else.

The out-patient therapy was continuing and I was on a new type of drug, an anti-depressant. Sometimes I even felt normal. Through therapy, I was even able to get back into touch with my mother. My father had died a few years back. It was very hard to deal with my dad's death. There were so many things I never got to say. It was hard for me to remember now what it was like growing up with him. I was his pride and joy. We were so close. I had so many dreams and ambitions. One event changed all that. He lived the rest of his life with disappointment and disowning his only child.

They never got over my giving my baby or Catherine (as she is now) to the Sisters. She had gone to another family immediately. They just couldn't seem to forgive me. Even when I had my two children with Peter, they would barely speak to me. Finally, I came to understand that they couldn't establish a relationship with me only to possibly have it ripped away again. Once I came to terms with that and my mother was free of my father's tyranny after his death, our relationship improved. She became an outrageous grandmother, wearing spandex and going to car races. The kids adored her. From the brief contact I've had with Catherine, I would like to think that it is my mom whom she resembles.

Catherine

Jeff took me to dinner at the Chatham Wayside Inn. It sat in the middle of Chatham's old village charm. Built in 1860 as a sea captain's home, the inn and restaurant has been exquisitely renovated and expanded to include fifty-six guest rooms. The dining was excellent, whether on the patio, in the pub, or in the fireside dining room. The menu featured fresh local seafood with a contemporary flair, as Chatham was still a major fishing port with a history that began in the mid 1600s. He ordered an incredible Cabernet Sauvignon, and we spoke of everything. He was so experienced in life, and I was a little in awe of him. He was so suave, so handsome. He ordered for me, and we had an incredible meal. We ended it with Cognac which I hadn't tried before, but at $50 per glass this stuff was smooth. When we went outside, it was pouring. Our car was rather far, and he offered to get it but I was fine walking with him. I was not a vain person.

His house was close, and we stopped so he could show it to me and change into dry clothes. He gave me some jeans and a T-shirt to wear since my dress was completely soaked.

He had impeccable taste. The house was modern and without the touch of a woman, but I was still impressed. The sound of the rain, the crickets, the candlelight and sitting on his couch, sipping coffee was very relaxing and comfortable.

He was a nice man but there wasn't any chemistry. Also, he wasn't Anthony, and I didn't think I could settle for anyone else.

At some point, I ran into a mutual friend who said they had heard from Anthony. Apparently, his parents had invited her, Jennie, to the reunion, not knowing he had met me. He hadn't mentioned me because he had been burned before and wanted to really make a go of us before he introduced me to his parents. He had also moved too quickly in previous relationships and wanted to handle this one slowly. He was upset that I hadn't believed in him. If there wasn't trust, there couldn't be a relationship.

The next day I had a bouquet of hydrangeas left at my door. They were large, round blasts of amethyst. They have always been my favorite and only one person knows this. Anticipation fills my chest but I quickly brushed it away. I looked around and saw no one. I hurried inside, change my clothes and went for a run. I needed to think some things over.

Sharon

I received a letter today. I didn't recognize the handwriting. I turned it over and over. There was no return address on it. I opened it with foreboding.

The letter read:

> I know I am a bother to you, but I think you owe me. You owe me information. There are some things I need to know.
>
> First, I want to know who my father is. Second, I want to know my medical history. I have a right to know this. Then I'll leave you alone.
>
> I don't want any money from you if that's what you're worried about, I just want answers. I wasted my whole life dreaming we were just alike. I was sure of it. I may look like you but I will never be like you! I waited by the phone every birthday for you to call. Did you ever think of me?
>
> Catherine

I have been feeling more anxious lately. I was feeling so well for a while that I stopped taking my anti-depressants. I thought *I'm fine. I don't need to take drugs.* My therapist advised against it, but I didn't listen. I actually stopped seeing her, also. I was sure I could continue this on my own.

I finished reading the letter, went into my bed, and pulled the covers up over my head. I closed my eyes and let myself wander to the comfortable state of unawareness: sleep.

Catherine

I came home from work and checked my messages. One call was a surprise.

"Hey, it's Anthony. I think we've had time to cool and I want to talk to you. I miss you. I hope you got the flowers I left. Call me."

It was hard to explain the feeling of hope and excitement mixed with foreboding. It was like coming home after a long trip and sinking into bed. I loved him. Should I call? Was it all his fault? He really was like other men, and I had thought he was different. How could I ever trust him? I didn't even know him. Was the breakup partly my fault? I looked at so many different angles.

I picked up the phone. Hung it up. Picked it up again. I dialed.

"Hello...."

"Hey, Deb. Want to meet me for a drink? I need to get the hell out of here before I lose my mind."

Deb was one of my best friends whom I met on Cape. She was an amazing person with infinite wisdom. We met at the Red Nun in Chatham. We ordered drinks and appetizers. We both received a few appreciative glances from men in the bar but ignored them. There was a small crowd at the bar, and everyone seemed to be enjoying themselves. Deb interrupted my thoughts.

"If you have any doubt, you will regret it later. At least let him explain. Maybe it's a big misunderstanding. Wouldn't you feel better making an informed decision about the man of your dreams versus just reacting to what it appears to be?"

Deb had this annoying way of making you look at your behavior and seeing it as ridiculous, which it usually is. She helped you to see both sides instead of immediately going to your corner. She was the mediator of relationships. Subconsciously, maybe that's why I called her.

After the third margarita, I headed to the ladies room while she asked for the check. As I came around the corner, I smashed right into a man coming into the bar from the lobby. As I looked up to apologize, I stumbled, not sure if I did from the tequila or the shock. He grabbed my arm and asked if I was all right.

"Fate keeps crashing us into each other it seems." He said in that womanizer voice of his.

"I'm sorry. Excuse me." I made it to the ladies room more as a haven now. He followed me in there. In an effort to avoid an intense conversation when I was not in a good state of mind, I kissed him. He rebuked my advances and grabbed me by the shoulders. "No. I followed you in here to talk to you."

The humiliation I felt at that moment- It was like the beating all over again. *No one will ever love you.* I still was not good enough, I still wouldn't be able to make him happy and I was the lowest of low. I looked at him and wasn't sure what I saw in his eyes. I knew he wanted to make sure we were on the same page but I still wasn't prepared for that conversation. With what little dignity I had left, I grabbed my purse and got the hell out of there.

Catherine

Jeff was, of course, at the annual autumn bash, being our number one donator. He asked to take me to dinner. After working so hard all day, I said yes, partly out of spite. I hadn't heard from Anthony since I had run into him. Jeff was pursuing me rather aggressively. Earlier that week, he sent me a beautiful poem on thick, expensive paper.

Come Slowly

by Emily Dickinson

Come slowly, Eden
Lips unused to thee.
Bashful, sip thy jasmines,
As the fainting bee,
Reaching late his flower,
Round her chamber hums,
Counts his nectars -alights,
And is lost in balms!

Jeff followed me home so I could get some things, and we drove to his house. He encouraged me to swim in his pool or sit in the Jacuzzi while he prepared dinner. I changed into the swimsuit I had brought and did some laps. It was still warm. I came up from under water, and he was at the pool's edge with a margarita in hand, salted on the rocks, the way I like it.

"I loved the poem. It was a nice surprise in a tough week." I said as I thanked him for the drink.

"I'm glad. I enjoy doing things for you. You're easy to please." He replied.

I laughed. The irony. It's weird how you can have different effects on people. One thing I had never been was easy in any sense.

He was making Cajun shrimp over a bed of Spanish rice. It smelled great. We ate outside as the sun set and the moon rose across the darkening sky. Our conversation was easy as always. It was comfortable being there with him. There was no pretense, just good company. He challenged me in every way intellectually, and we bantered back and forth late into the night. But I knew I couldn't love him back. After a while, he drove me home.

That was the last time I saw him.

Catherine, 1993

The surf pounded against the shore. The waves steadily came and then crashed like lovers' broken promises, coming close and then pulling away. I was sitting near the edge of the sand where it met the reaching hands of the dark, angry ocean. The water was creeping up with each break, testing. It was like my life….push and push….how far can I be pushed? The Atlantic touched my toes and it was warm. It felt warmer than the air tonight. The double latte that I had brought with me didn't seem to be warming me up.

I felt the world lift off my shoulders as I inhaled and walked. It was one of those nights that I could wander these shores forever. I was one with the ocean tonight. It's vastness reminded me of the smallness of my life…of my problems. It also reminded me of Anthony. These nooks of the Cape were ours: the Chatham Fishing Pier where we talked for hours and watched the fishermen bring in their catch; Kevin's, where we found the Cape's best chowder; Boardwalk beach in Sandwich where we collected smooth stones. Everywhere I looked he was there. My heart ached for him. The heaviness returned to my chest.

I believed in fate. I've never believed in a god, but I've always believed things happen for a reason. I tried so hard to tell myself that this past year's heartache was worth it. Something good had to happen soon.

I walked some more. It was low tide and I was at the opening of Swan River. We had kayaked here once, and the weather turned. The kayak tipped way off shore, near Bomber's Island, and I was panicking in the deep, dark water. I just kept thinking of sharks. There was a sighting close to shore around the elbow of the Cape from where we were. I was kicking and thought that would signal the sharks but somehow couldn't stop thrashing. Anthony made me focus on him and talked me through it. We couldn't get the boat up side right and had to swim all the way in. He waved down a windsurfer to bring me in. He just wanted me safe. I just couldn't help but wonder: How do we know? What path do we take? What if it was the wrong one and we regret it?

I stood out on the sand bar for a while contemplating. The sun had set- it was time to go home. I turned to walk back. The beach was empty but for one solitary elderly women and her dog. We smiled at each other as we passed.

"Nice dog," I said. She thanked me. She started speaking to me. She told me she and her husband lived on Longell Ave for 30 years, and he had passed away two weeks ago. His dog was all she had left. She was sobbing. I stood there awkwardly, wondering what had made this stranger open up to me like that. I felt sorry for her. I wondered what her life had been like and tried to picture what she looked like at my age. At least she had been able to spend that time with someone she loved. But now what? What will she do now? It must seem hopeless for someone that late in life- do you go on or just wait to die? We spoke some more. Then I expressed my condolences and continued on my way. But I couldn't help consider the quick life we live and looking back at her age, was there regret or had she lived life the way she truly wanted? The one thing I remembered feeling as I walked away was how I needed to live my best life- one that was right for me.

I turned the corner of the marsh grass, and there was another solitary figure. It was funny how the ocean drew us the way the moon rules the tide. I was always hesitant to leave. The silhouette stood out amidst the oncoming darkness. There was something familiar about it that made me hesitate….it could have been the way he held himself, it could have been his gait.

It was Anthony! He, too, was standing on the edge of the water- not far from where I was originally. Was this my answer? My heart literally dropped before I could find the words. I didn't need to because at that moment he turned.

His eyes get me all the time. They looked right past me and deep into my soul, and he knew. He knew it was our time. I was ready to talk and commit myself to him. We knew we both wanted this. This time it would work. I wouldn't run away.

Sharon, 1995

I awoke today and felt that familiar sadness pulling me back down. I was disappointed. I had thought I could escape it. It was like being tied to a heavy weight under water. I could see the light above but I could never quite reach it. I dragged the weight, stirring up clouds of dust, and fought against it, but it kept me down. When I finally opened my eyes, I didn't see the sun shining in the sky. I didn't hear the birds singing. I saw another hopeless day-the vastness of another day to remind me of failure. I heard my own voice berating me, telling me that I have not only made bad choices that have ruined my life but those of others.

I kept the shades closed as I have made it my habit of late. I stumbled into the bathroom, turned on the light, and looked in the mirror. I noticed my Hawaiian streak of white looked more gray. I noticed the lines around my eyes and my mouth from years of frowning.

There was no sparkle there. There was dullness, an emptiness in the shell of a person looking back at me. I was finally able to remember who I was as a child and compare it against what I have become. I looked into that mirror for a long time. I felt aching regret. It was the end of September and I was close to 40 now.

I gritted my teeth and screamed inside *I can't do this anymore!* It was so real that I felt every fiber of my being was screaming and I wondered if the screams were out loud. I would give in to it. I was tired of collapsing into depression, year after year, after year. I had no fight left.

I listened closely and heard silence. I didn't even know what time it was but I knew that Bill was at work and Donna and Steve were living their own lives. I was alone- I laughed- literally and figuratively. It was then that I wept. I felt a relief. It was pouring out of me. The way your eyes swell up until they cannot hold anymore and finally that first drop was released and it was like a flood. I felt that first tear run down my cheek. I could feel gravity pulling it down, the way it pulled at my entirety.

When I was done, I was calm. There was a peacefulness in my face as I took one last look. The decision was made easily. I grabbed the almost full bottle of anti-depressants that I never finished when I took myself off them the last time. I grabbed a glass of tap water. Then I purposefully walked into my room with the darkness of the pulled shades that matched the darkness of my heart.

Catherine, 1995

It was a beautiful fall day. The first of October. We had chosen a Bed and Breakfast in New England with a wrap-around farmer's porch. It was peak foliage at the Harrington Inn in Princeton, Massachusetts. I was just applying a final touch of lipstick when I heard my cue- Fly Me to the Moon had started to play and the violin sound was echoing throughout the peak foliage mountain-side. We had 50 guests waiting for us – waiting for me to walk down the decorated field. It has been a long journey, but we had finally found our way back. He was patient and let me find myself because he knew it would make us stronger. I now knew that I needed to go through what I did. Everything was incomplete for so long, and it took me so long to realize what I now knew.

People were waiting, but there was one more thing I needed to do before Anthony and I got married. I grabbed a pen from the table and wrote on the inn's advertising postcards:

"There's more to me than you."

It was addressed to Sharon Szaban. I asked the inn keeper to mail it. Then I took Shane's arm as I started walking down the aisle to my soon-to be-husband and never looked back at the "what-ifs."